A Beauty By Its Blue Reflection

Neelima Rajawat

First Published in 2021

Becomeshakespeare.com
One Point Six Technologies Pvt. Ltd.
119-123, 1st Floor, Building J2, B - Wing,
Wadala Truck Terminal, Wadala East,
Mumbai 400022, Maharashtra, INDIA
T: +91 8080226699

ISBN - 978-93-5438-058-7

Dedication

This book is dedicated to
my late Dadaji who believed me!

Acknowledgment

I would like to express my special thanks of gratitude to my late Dadaji and Agrawal sir. Where my Dadaji taught me life lessons, Agrawal sir taught me so many academic theories.

Thanks to my parents who kept inspiring me while I was writing this book. Most importantly, I want to say thanks to all the characters of this book inspired by my beloved friends who made it interesting.

To Readers,

Thanks for choosing A *Beauty By Its Blue Reflection*. As you chose my book over leaving all your work and social activities.

It is not only the book, it is a combination of different phases of lives. If someone's struggle and learning phases are helpful in someone else's life, then it's amazing & helpful.

Preface

A Beauty By Its Blue reflection is the humble attempt to open up the life of an Indian girl fictionally.

This book is a fictional story of the 27 years life of Neelima, who is the main character of this book. Here, things are written about different phases of life with different perceptions of a single thought. A life journey, till 2020, is from beginning to a successful life. This book includes tiny-tales of the ups and downs of life. Everyone has different stories and different learning phases in their lives. Someone's life can be influential and a lot of learning stages can help others to tackle similar situations in their lives. All stories written in this book can make you happy, sad, inspired, adorable, and independent. This book is full of logic as written by a Software engineer.

Blue Reflection is a role-playing game, which follows a day cycle. The player takes the role of Hinako Shirai, a ballet dancer who due to a knee injury no longer can dance, but who is given magical power allowing her to fight and move freely. Here, I tried to relate the life of Neelima with the life of the game character Hinako Shirai. In her life, Neelima also struggled and tried to stand for herself and more freely. The purpose is to motivate and inspire people for struggling in their lives for achieving something.

The meaning of Neelima is a beauty by its blue reflection. Beauty can be shown after the dispersion of blue color in the sky. Why is the sky *blue*? Blue light is scattered more than the other colors because it travels as shorter, smaller waves but higher frequencies. Therefore, we see a blue sky most of the time. Another motivation is to spread yourself, open all your options, and try to get what you like with own your efforts.

Along with that blue is the only color which maintains its own character in all its tones it will always stay blue. According to me, it's quite motivating and like the character of the book. Always stay with what you are. No need to be fake for showing others. It's your life so live it for yourself and the way you like it.

As being a software engineer, I tried to write this book in a pattern as we develop a software which we use to call waterfall model which goes through several phases like analysis, design, coding testing, & maintenance. So here, I considered life as software and has written the book as making different phases of life one after the other.

Last but not the least, why index of chapters is started with 0 and numbers are written inside the square brackets? because in basic computer programming languages array index use to start with zero. Although Zero is one of the turning points of Neelima's s life.

About the Author

Neelima Rajawat is working as an engineer in a product based Multinational company. She is NITian, Karma Believer, & Engineer. She has pursued her master's from the National Institute of Technology, Hamirpur. Along with that, she is a self-made, hardworking, and motivational person who never says no to anything.

LinkedIn:

http://linkedin.com/in/neelima-rajawat-03b96b93

Facebook:

https://www.facebook.com/rajawatneelima

Email:

rajawatneelima3@gmail.com

Facebook page:

https://www.facebook.com/Neelima-Rajawat-105369584888831/?refid=17

Contents

[0]

The Beginning

2005-2011

Today is September 3, 2020. Right now, I am in Hyderabad and it's raining here. I was playing a game with Alexa.

Who is Alexa?

Amazon Alexa, also known simply as Alexa, is a virtual assistant AI technology developed by Amazon. It was first used in the Amazon Echo smart speakers developed by Amazon Lab126.

These days this device is an important part of my daily life. So, I started commanding Alexa to continue my game.

Me: Alexa, open Akinator!

Alexa: Hi, I am Akinator, and I can read your mind. Think of a character and I will try to guess. Are you ready?

Me: Yes!

Then I thought about one character in my mind. After that, Alexa started asking questions like is your character male or female? Does your character belong to Bollywood or Hollywood? And I was answering in yes or no. While I was just busy playing and diverting my mind with Alexa, the whole world was trapped in a pandemic situation because of Novel Coronavirus disease (COVID-19).

HOW COVID IS SPREADING

The virus, which is causing COVID-19 is mainly transmitted through droplets generated when an infected person coughs, sneezes, or touches. These droplets are assumed to be too heavy to hang in the air, and quickly fall on floors or surfaces.

People are getting infected by breathing in the virus if they are within close proximity of someone who has COVID-19, or by touching a contaminated surface and then eyes, nose, or mouth.

HOW COVID-19 STARTED

Coronavirus disease (COVID-19) is defined as an illness caused by a novel coronavirus, now called severe acute respiratory syndrome coronavirus 2 (SARS-CoV-2). In December 2019, this disease was first identified amid an outbreak of respiratory illness cases in Wuhan City, Hubei Province, China.

It was initially reported to the WHO on December 31, 2019. On January 30, 2020, the WHO declared the COVID-19 outbreak a global health emergency. On March 11, 2020, the WHO declared COVID-19 a global pandemic.

On 24 March 2020, Narendra Modi with the Government of India ordered a nationwide lockdown for 21 days, limiting the movement of the entire 1.3 billion population of India as a preventive measure against the COVID-19 pandemic in India. The lockdown was placed when the number of confirmed positive coronavirus cases in India was approximately 500.

After getting Indians to bang pots and pans on their balconies on March 22, 2020, to show their appreciation for the doctors, nurses, and others on the frontline of the battle against Covid-19, Prime Minister Narendra Modi appeared on television on Friday to ask his fellow citizens to light candles and switch on mobile flashlights for nine minutes on April 5, 2020, to mark the fight against the disease. Then as per Narendra Modi's instructions, we all lighten lamps.

However, as the time of ending the first lockdown was nearing, the government prolonged it for a longer period. On April 14, 2020, Prime minister Narendra Modi extended the nationwide lockdown until May 3, 2020, with conditional relaxations.

On May 1, 2020, the Government of India protracted the nationwide lockdown further by two weeks until May 17,

2020. The Government divided all the districts into three zones based on the spread of the virus—green, red and orange—with relaxations applied accordingly. On May 17, 2020, the lockdown was further extended till May 31, 2020, by the National Disaster Management Authority.

On May 30, 2020, it was announced that the lockdown restrictions were to be lifted from then onwards, while the ongoing lockdown would be further extended till June 30, 2020, for only the containment zones. Services would be resumed in a phased manner starting from June 8, 2020.

Unlock 1.0

It was termed as "Unlock 1.0". The Prime Minister later clarified that the lockdown phase in the country was over and that 'unlock' had already begun.

Unlock 2.0

Unlock 2.0, was announced for the period of 1 to 31 July, with more ease in restrictions.

Unlock 3.0

Unlock 3.0 was announced for August.

Unlock 4.0

Unlock 4.0 was announced for September.

Because of this pandemic situation, I don't feel safe going out. I don't have any other option due to Covid19 so I can not go out and chill like before. So just scrolling news feeds and thinking about the current situation of India due to this disease, when we would get a vaccine? will we all be free like before?

In between, I heard some sound that instantly diverted my attention. Oh! I got one new WhatsApp notification on my phone. I unlocked it and opened WhatsApp. Yeah, I could see that message is from Naman!

Since 2017, Naman has been my friend from the same hometown. He is like my brother but he's not my brother. In the starting Naman and I used to play a GK game named:

"THE TEST"

In this game, we get an alternate chance of answering the question. We were very fond of this game as we both thought ourselves the most genius person for answering.

He is my good friend who always comes with his broken stories. Yeah..! because I am a good motivator sometimes. So I used to tell him different ways to heal himself from stress when you are broken. That's how we were connected after having a lot of meaningful conversations on social issues as he was studying sociology.

In the beginning, we used to have conversations through messages and calls only but whenever I travelled to Delhi We used to meet at ISBT McDonald's in Delhi.

During my masters, I travelled from Gwalior to NITH by crossing Delhi. I used to travel from Gwalior to Delhi by train, then from Delhi to NITH by bus. To take the bus I needed to go from Delhi railway station to **Inter-State Bus Terminus** (ISBT) at Kashmere Gate in Delhi. At ISBT McDonald's he used to speak about his stories and I used to eat **Brownie** with **Ice cream**!

Once I was travelling from Gwalior to NITH, so when I reached Delhi I was so hungry but as I had Bus so I tried to reach ISBT just after reaching outstation. Naman also came to ISBT and we met at the same place.

Me: Hey bro! I am so hungry, let's eat something.

Naman: What would you like to have?

Me: I would like to have a meal and what about you?

Naman: I won't eat anything as I am on a keto diet.

Me: Hey, at least have some drink only.

Naman: Ok, then I will take one coffee. Let me go and place the order.

Me: No, let me do it. I will pay for us.

Naman: No, this time let me do. Next time you can pay.

Then he paid for our orders because this is the guy who always pays. After some time, I got my meal and I was continuously eating as I was so hungry. Again Naman was telling his broken story. So I was listening to his story while eating. After some time when he was in the middle of his story, I interrupted him.

Me: Hey, Naman, I am feeling to have one Mcfloat for me. Let me go and take it.

Naman: Wait, I will get it for you, till then you finish whatever is left with you.

Then Naman went and bought Mcfloat for me and I was eating and he continued his story. So that's how we used to meet and share all our stories.

Today also he is supposed to ping me either for telling something or for knowing something. As per my expectations, here also he was trying to know something:

Naman: Do you have a boyfriend?

I was thinking why Naman is curious about my stuff? Why did this question come to me? Then I replied to him.

Me: No, I am not interested in having dogs.

Then again he asked another question:

Naman: What do you look for in a dog?

then I took a breath and little pause and thought for some time then replied to him as:

Me: Actually, I am interested in equality in society and a person's mind and deeds not only in a statement.

Then he replied as:

Naman: Good luck for equality and a person's mind.

That's how we ended the conversation. It was so rude to him but for now, I have become a person like this because of my past circumstances.

I am Neelima. Yes, I live in a country where boys remain prized, and having a daughter is considered to be an imprecation by so many. Many are not so fortunate, and I am one of those who faced the same situations.

In Indian society, women are traditionally discriminated against and excluded from political and family-related decisions. Despite the large amount of work women must do daily to support their families, their opinions are rarely acknowledged and their rights are limited.

The status of women in India has been subject to many changes throughout recorded Indian history. Their position in society deteriorated early in India's ancient period, especially in the Indo-Aryan speaking regions, and their subordination continued to be reified well into India's early modern period. Practises such as female infanticide, dowry, child marriage and the taboo on widow remarriage, which began in upper-caste Hindu society in Northern India, have had a long duration, proving difficult to root out, and in the instance of dowry have spread to all castes, classes, and even religions.

Rani Lakshmi Bai, the Queen of Jhansi, led the Indian Rebellion of 1857 against the British. She is now widely considered a national hero.

The wage gap between Indian men and women is the gender pay gap that is still quite wide. According to the Monster Salary Index (MSI) published in March 2019, women in the country earn 19% less than men. The survey revealed that the median gross hourly salary for men in India in 2018 was ₹242.49, while ₹196.3 for women, meaning men earned ₹46.19 more than women.

According to the survey, the gender pay gap spans across key industries. IT services showed a sharp pay gap of 26% in favour of men, while in the manufacturing sector, men earn 24% more than women. Different laws have been established for the sake of women.

Have you ever thought about what it would be like if girls and boys were raised equally despite their physical differences? Since the very beginning of childhood, there has been a different set of rules for girls and for boys, there are 'almost no rules'. Society sets standards for girls in every walk of life – dress properly, talk slowly, sit nicely, don't drink or smoke, come home on time, behave yourself in public but all this is not relevant when you are raising a boy. Yes because, "you are a boy", whatever they do at home and in public – they have a shield for it.

Can we do our bit to change the way we bring up our boys and girls? Tell the boys that they cannot just escape whenever they do something which reflects their so-called 'manhood' at home or in public. Tell the girls that they cannot simply bow down and let the boys take advantage of their 'womanhood' – neither at home nor in public.

In a country where over 80 percent of the population worships Goddesses of different kinds, the status of women and what they represent has varied greatly from ancient to modern times. In Vedic society, women had the same status as men in all aspects of life.

Rightly did Swami Vivekanand say, 'Just as a bird cannot fly with one wing only, a Nation cannot march forward if the women are left behind'. Men and women are the two holes of a perfect whole. Strength is borne of their union; their separation results in weakness. Each has what the other does not have. Each completes the other and is completed by the other. Etymologically, the word 'woman' means half of a man.

The relation of the male and female is very well illustrated in our Nyaya Darshan by the analogy of mind and matter, which means that man and woman are closely associated with each other, as the soul and body. Therefore, the women ought to be respected.

I don't understand why there is no equality for women? Why women are not treated equally. Although in this modern India, people used to give so many statements socially and politically but inside their minds and houses, things are still similar. Why so many rules for girls only not for boys. What if boys stop doing what scares girls? Why are they not brought up like this?

We worship Maha Lakshmi, Saraswati and Durga so devotedly every morning for wealth, knowledge, happiness, etc. But when a female child is born in the family, people refuse to welcome the little angel into their homes. Despite the government's much-hyped policy of 'Beti Bachao, Beti Padhao', the negative attitude towards the girl child is deeply rooted in the Indian psyche.

Let me start how things came up for me in Indian society after explaining about this society and people's mindset.

How I got the chance to come into this world

Apparently, my parents got to know about me when pregnancy was in a non-terminated stage. Else I would have been aborted. By God's grace, I came into this world.

After my birth, no one including my parents was happy as I was their unwanted child. Because my parents were expecting a boy and they got a girl. My mom didn't even eat anything for the next 2-3 days as she had given birth to a girl.

For so many years relatives and all used to laugh at me because I was unwanted and useless to my own parents. My mom didn't even look after me. When I grew older then also she was never interested in me.

I never got that love and care which every child gets from their parents. Seeing so many rejections and hate since my childhood, I had decided to become my parent's most wanted child. As no one was happy so no one used to celebrate my birthday.

I used to spend my days with Grandpa and grandma. Whenever I wanted something or wanted to talk about something then every time I used to do it with my grandparents only. Once I saw everyone was getting anklets from their parents but I didn't get them. I was so hurt while seeing that no one was there for me.

I used to sleep with my grandma so one day I just hugged her and requested:

"Could you please ask grandpa to buy anklets for me.?"

Then the next day itself she asked grandpa regarding my anklets. After some days, I finally got my anklets. I can still recollect they both loved me a lot. Wherever they're... still I feel annexed with them.

So when I had completed my six years then I had commenced going to the same primary government school in which my mom used to teach those days. So that's how I started my schooling.

In my village, we had two separate houses in front of each other. So in one house all men used to live and in another one all the women. My mom used to live in a house that was for women but after coming to school I used to stay in another house with my grandparents as I felt scared with my mom because she never talked to me well. Every time she only screamed at me. It was authentically horrible staying with her.

After some years, my brother and parents; "son" came into the world. My parents and the whole family were so happy even I was so happy as I got someone to play with me. So I started doing things with my brother only. At his birth, my brother got one cradle for him. After one or two years he got one small scooter of purple colour with three wheels and two paddles attached with that. So I used to ride that scooter by taking my brother in the back seat. As we both shared a good bond. Then I also started getting some good time with my parents.

When I had learned to read Hindi books then one day I was reading one Hindi story in my book. At that time I read people were praising a girl because she did something great. I got inspired by that story and asked all to change my name in the school. That's how I chose things and became Neelima.

Every year I used to see everyone was celebrating the birthdays of all the boys in the house. But no one ever celebrated any girl's birthday. Even though I was a child, some thoughts came into my mind. I was thinking:

"We all are human beings. We all are taking birth and we all are dying everything is identically tantamount. Then why is this partiality? Why is this differentiation?

Then I talked with my grandma. She wasn't able to answer my questions, but she promised me to celebrate my birthday.

My First B'day celebration:

My b'day was about to come so I asked my grandma to prepare a cake for me. As per my request, she made barfi and set it on the plate like a cake then we decorated it by using flower pellets. Also, I had purchased three long balloons as at that time I used to have only some coins in my pocket money.

On the birthday, after setting up all the things like hanging those three balloons and keeping one candle in that cake (Barfi) made by my grandma. Then we called grandpa. When grandpa came after seeing all the settings he got a little excited. He said, "Call Saket".

In those decades, we didn't have mobile phones or cameras. For every occasion, we used to call Saket. Saket was the Photographer and our neighbour. Then I cut the cake and so many pics had been clicked. That's how I celebrated my first birthday. I got some rupees as a gift.

In the village, I used to go to school and I was a sharp-minded student and my grandpa was a Mathematics teacher so he used to teach me maths and science. I had completed my 5th board exam from the same village government school itself.

Whenever I wanted to go shopping in the town near the village, I used to go with grandpa on his bicycle. so many efforts at that age he used to do for me.

On 15th august occasion of independence day, we used to perform something in school where all village schools combined one show that had been conducted in the big ground of the village that was little far from my village. Once in that show I recited a poem which was written and composed by Hariom Pawar:

"Kashmir jo khud Suraj ek bête ki Rajdhani tha,

Damru wale shiv Shankar ki jo ghati kalyani tha"

After hearing this poem by me, I got so many applauses from the audience. It was a great honour. We used to receive some awards based on our performance. At that time, I got first prize and in that first prize, one small table clock of pink color was given to me. I was so happy by getting the first reward of my life. I used to put this clock with me and started waking up by keeping the alarm in this.

So before reciting this poem, I needed to dictate some lines regarding the poem but before starting itself I forgot those four lines. Then the public had started screaming at me

"Just start your poem and leave those headlines."

So I did the same. Actually which lines were given by my father one day before independence day over the call. Yeah, that time we used to have landline phones. So I couldn't remember those lines in public due to so much pressure.

Then, I came to the 5th standard. At that time 5th standard was board examination. So I prepared hard with the help of my grandpa as he helped me a lot for understanding mathematics questions and science theory, which was part of the syllabus. In the village, during night times we used to lighten up lanterns and lamps by filling kerosene oil in those. During nights, I used to study in the light of lanterns.

In the afternoon and evening, I used to do household chores with my grandma. Yeah, I can make perfect round shape chapati because I learned that with my grandma. There are a lot of things that I learned from my grandma.

In the 5th standard, I used to study with my best friend Ranu. After 5th class board exams, She said:

"I am going to join the city school, what are your plans?"

Then I replied, " I will talk to my grandpa. based on that we will decide."

Then I told everything to my grandparents that Rano was going to join the city school so I also wanted to go to the city school. After that, they talked with my father regarding this and my father got convinced.

Beginning of Modern Life

Since my childhood, I was a struggling person, but my real struggle had started from 6th standard. When I came to the city for further study, in the entrance exam of a city school, I failed in English although I passed in mathematics and science with the help of my sister as she helped me a lot. As I came from the village so those days I was only a piece of shit, people used to laugh at me because I was so naïve in this modern world.

After the exam, when the entrance test result came, and dad got to know that I didn't pass the entrance test then anyhow he convinced the principal of the school for my admission in the same school with my sister. Before school started, I got my sixth class books for those books dad brought covers and he asked me to put the cover on all the books so that these could be reliable. For setting covers on the books, I needed to fix it by using pins. So I tried to punch pins by using a stapler. It was my first time when I was using a stapler. So what I did instead of punching pins on the book I punched it in both of my first fingers. It was horrible when it started bleeding from both of my fingers and after seeing this I started crying. My brother heard this so he ran out to me and also called all and so they came to the study room and helped me in removing pins from my fingers. After some time when I stopped crying then all were laughing at me. As before this, I was in the village so I wasn't aware of all these basic things before.

So, after all this, we both started going to school. Well my school was inside the small streets and in a small constructed area although it was one of the best schools in the town.

The principal of the school was the owner as well as the best English teacher. we used to call him Agrawal sir. He was very strict & punctual. He was very old but still, he could do anything like brooming and mopping in the school. That's how great people behave. I really liked Agrawal sir as a person.

I started going to school with my sister & I was in 6th class and my sister was in 7th class. So, we used to go to school by walking from the old railway track. I was so focused on studying. It was like I used to remember theories line by line and also I was able to tell page numbers too.

Then it was the time of the quarterly exam result time. When my sister and I came from school, dad was asking about my sister's result as she was a brilliant student then she said check Neelima's result. She also topped in her class, so dad was shocked as he didn't expect this from me. So, this was the beginning where I stepped out for the first time to prove myself.

As I had started living in the city so in this modern world every other girl's birthday had been celebrated by their family. So I expected that my birthday would also be celebrated by my parents. Because I used to go to my classmates' birthday parties with a small bouquet and one good reasonable pen as a gift. Birthday rules:

1.   Distribute chocolates in the class.

2.   Gift small bouquet with one good pen

3.   Cut the cake and serve the food.

So on my birthday, I invited my classmates in the morning while I went to school but when I came back to home then I saw no one was even interested in celebrating my birthday along with that my mom denied to cook food for my friends. As I had already invited them so I couldn't even do anything

After knowing all this and seeing my family's reactions, I just started crying because they had already celebrated my sister's birthday a few months ago but at my time things were totally different. The second thought which was coming into my mind was what I would say to my friends when they come. My dad saw me crying then he came to me

Dad: What happened? Why are you crying

Me: Today is my birthday and no one is doing anything for me.

Dad: Oh! Seriously today's your birthday.

Me: Yes, it's today only and I already invited my friends.

Dad: So what's the problem. We will do things the way we have done on your sister's birthday.

Me: But How? Mom was saying she won't do anything.

Dad: Let me talk with her.

Literally that day I cried almost for 2 hours on my birthday because of this weird behaviour of my family for me. I didn't understand what I did, what was the fault. So after some discussion and arguments with mom dad came back to my room and started as:

Dad: Give me a bag. I will go to the market and will purchase food and birthday cake from there because mom is not getting ready.

This was a very shocking thing for me because from this age I had started understanding this differentiation between me and my siblings. Although I could have celebrated my birthday because of my dad. So things were handled anyhow.

Because of all these small incidents I totally become a different person. After that, I was not so good in behavior and looks because I used to look slim and dark. So, because of my color, look and behavior no one liked me. In school, I didn't talk much as I felt low confidence even though I was the topper of the class.

In all three exams (quarterly, half-yearly and finals) I used to score rank 1. I used to get out of marks in almost three subjects out of six along with 10%-15% more than my classmates. I was that noob as I didn't even talk with anyone during classes.

I was doing good in my academics but still, I wasn't happy because every time family members used to tell me that "I am unwanted" so I have also started feeling, I am good for nothing. Because I was raised with this feeling, so I became irritated and worse in behavior.

On one Sunday evening, I was playing badminton outside of my house then suddenly I fell down and my leg got fractured. The same day, dad came late and I had to bear the pain till the next day when we will go to the doctor.

The next day dad took me to the government hospital as that time we were not so financially stable because parents were government teachers on a small basic salary. In the hospital, one doctor just checked and asked for plaster as it got fractured so. Then after holding plaster on my leg I was going out with my dad then suddenly one known person to dad came and started talking with him. In between their conversation, he asked my dad:

"How many kids do you have?"

Then dad replied confidently that

"I've only one daughter and one son. This girl is my brother's daughter, not mine."

At that time I was in 7th standard, not so much older. My age was 12-13 years old. After hearing this I was like why? Where's me? What's my identity? I don't even exist in this world. So many thoughts suddenly came into my mind like:

- Maybe I don't look good.

- Maybe I am not her daughter in real life.

- Maybe he picked me from some garage box.

- Maybe he feels shameful while telling others about me.

7th Standard:

Now, I came into the 7th standard. We all were taking classes and suddenly we heard something,

may I come in, sir?

Oh, one new admission about which we all classmates only heard, asked this question. So this new student is a girl.

After talking some days we got to know her name. Her name was Sriya. After some days Sriya became one of my good friends. She used to sit next to me. This sitting arrangement used to be made by principal Sir who was the owner of the school and English teacher.

Sriya was a very dangerous girl as she was outspoken about things whenever someone is saying something or bothering her she was paying off instantly to anyone for everything.

One day some of the classmates were hiding something from Sriya. Well, no one can do that, but still, they tried to do it. Then suddenly Sriya checked them hiding something so she asked them to show her but still they were not showing to her so she tried to snatch it and she got it.

Oh! It was a chewing gum pack. After getting it while Sriya was taking one chewing gum from that pack, she got an electric shock. Oops, that was Chewing Gum Electric Shock Gag Joke Toy.

Hahaha...! All my other classmates were laughing at her. They played with her and she got trapped. Although I like people like Sriya as she had all the qualities for being on my friend list.

One day my sister got a bicycle as a gift for going to school. Although I was good at cycling and I learned to ride before her, still she got it without even asking and before me and I didn't.

Since my childhood, for everything every day I needed to fight with everyone because I never got anything without asking.

I used to feel that "my sister is so lucky as every time she is getting things so easily ". She was very calm and kind towards everyone. On the other end, I had become rude, ruthless and violent. Every time I was only hated by my parents. Because of being unwanted and this feeling used to kill me from inside.

8th standard

Coming to my academics, well I was in 8th standard and at that time 8th was board. So Agrawal sir was very serious about teaching us English perfectly. So he used to teach us thoroughly about games. One day he organised a twenty minutes game. In that game, he gave one assignment where he spoke twenty tough English words which we all needed to write down correctly. There was a rule of 1 stick at 1 mistake. So we all classmates gave it a hard try to win this game.

On my turn, I got to know that I had written incorrect spelling of the word "usually". So all were whispering.

Neelima is the topper of the class, so Agrawal sir will leave her for sure.!

But nothing happened like this. In the end, everyone got sticks only. That's why I really liked Agrawal because he was always fair to everyone. He never made any differences between the topper and other classmates. The sitting arrangement was always decided by him and that was based on rank in the class.

Due to the board exams, the exam centre was out of school in some other school. That whole classmate and I used to go to that exam centre every day to appear in the exam. As

I was a topper since 6th class so when I came to the board exam everyone was very serious and everyone wanted to complete their exam perfectly.

So after some time, the whole class had started shouting Neelima please tell us, tell us... Neelima please tell us.!

Then invigilators came and we all again became silent. After some months when results came out then again I only topped. For prize distribution to the toppers, one of my dad's friends only came to my school, then by seeing a certificate he got to know his friend's daughter itself is getting a prize.

9th standard,

Here we got a computer in our home for the first time. It was black with an LCD. When I tried to use it for the first time instead of moving the mouse of the computer I tried to pick it up for moving onto the display screen. As this was my first time when I used a computer so I was naive and didn't even know how to use it. At the same time, my dad got a mobile phone for himself. So one day, dad forgot it on the table. Then it was ringing. When I tried to pick the call

I screamed just after holding it. Because it was vibrating and for the first time I felt something like that. It was so scary for a new person. That's what I could only say at that time.

Things were going on like this only and time had flown and came in 10th standard. As I was studying in the district's topmost school where every year students used to come in the top 20 merit list.

As I was the topper of the school from 6th standard, parents, school faculties had expectations as they wanted to see me in the top 5. When you are aware of people's expectations then instead of putting effort, you used to feel yourself with that burden. So, during my time, I felt like this so I couldn't perform better. Although I got good marks in all 5 subjects but in Hindi, I got only 69/100.

First cheque by state

Along with district topper, I was the first person from my district who got 99 marks in sanskrit. So the government rewarded me by a cheque. Basically sanskrit was the toughest language to write because we needed to remember so many forms and ways of writing those words. It strictly followed its grammar rules. It was very tough for me but still I did it. My dad praised me for this.So it was one of the happiest moments of my life.

WHY I went to court

After when the result came, dad filed a case that my Hindi copy wasn't checked properly. And in 11th class, I went to Gwalior High court. It was like watching movies; I was so excited as we were about to go in front of the judge to hear where he needed to show a Hindi copy. Then finally I saw my Hindi copy in court and I got to know that they just gave me marks in some pattern like if it's a question of 5 marks then I got 2 or 3 marks or if the question of 3 marks then I got 1 or 2 marks then the judge asked some questions to me.

Me: Although, I have written everything correctly but...

Judge: Ok, Neelima let me know your point.

Me: Evaluation has been done incorrectly.

Judge: Hindi copies are evaluated like this only. What's wrong with this?

Me: If a question is of 5 marks in that I got 2 or 3 marks or if a question is of 3 marks then I got 1 or 2 marks only.

Judge: If you are getting some scholarship somewhere then with your current total, you are already in the top 20 (if not in the top 10).

Me: Oh is it? Then it's fine.

After that, the case was closed. Later, I got a letter where they had declared that I got 17th rank in MP & according to that I was in the top 20 list of the state.

After 10th standard and all this, I had decided to change my medium as per my sister's suggestions. Till 10th standard, I studied in Hindi medium school and still I didn't get into the top ten list because of my Hindi marks so I thought to change my medium. In the beginning, my dad was not supporting this but when my sister talked then after some days he got convinced.

Things were going on. I needed to choose either mathematics or biology. With Mathematics in 11th standard, I have taken admission in English medium school in my town. So, I have completed my 11-12 from there. Yeah, in the beginning, it was very tough to understand the whole material in English, but I used to sit with a dictionary that's why covering up things was easy for me.

The blunder of my life

In 12th standard, I had an oreva scooter that worked by charging it So I used to go tuitions by my own vehicle but suddenly, at home some weird things had been started by my parents. Like, don't go there, don't do this, don't talk on calls, don't stand in front of the main door. Don't talk with boys. Lots of restrictions, because all time parents used to read and watch some weird news regarding girls like a girl is raped, a girl cheated his parents, a girl ran away with her lover and so on. Although my parents knew me since childhood, they still were behaving like this. At that time taking breaths was also the toughest task for me in that kind of environment.

After this mentality, my parents got another reason and came up with the same question which had been raised at my birth. Why give birth to a daughter if one day they're becoming a reason for shame. So parents behaviour had completely changed. At home, everything had become like torture and taunting.

Even though I was fully focused on my studies, I was bearing all this nonsense every day. After a lot of trials to make them understand that

"Everyone is not the same. As I am your child so you should have some faith in me."

But nothing had changed. One day they were continuously screaming for everything even I was doing right or wrong they were not even caring. They were just showing their frustration to me. So I lost all my control and came into my room locked the door from inside then immensely picked all out refill and drank it. At that time I wasn't able to see anything. After some time I got so scared that I would die and I didn't want to die so I told my brother that I drank All-out liquid. Then he ran away and told this to mom dad. They picked me and took me to the hospital. One of dad's friends and mom went to the hospital with me because dad didn't come with us because he didn't want to be trapped in any police case. So he tried to hide.

That's the modern world. Here, people are with you when you're productive for them. Else no one even cares about you dying.

After this incident, I decided to live for myself, not for anyone else. It was my life and I only needed to care about it.

Also, I realised that even if I would have died no one wouldn't even feel bad. So it would have been totally my loss only. So I had decided never to do that foolishness in my life again. After some days I had recovered.

After this, my brother used to play with me by saying that

"You have drunk mosquito repellent, now no mosquitoes would come closer to you."

After some months, we had forgotten that incident.

This life is very precious. We can do an abundance of things, we can learn a plethora of things. We can let so many people know what we know. So we should utilize our life instead of wasting it without even celebrating all this.

12th Standard

So, I came to the 12th standard. In 12th standard, one of the Physics faculty said, I don't know how you would pass the exams as per seeing your current status. We couldn't say anything.

After hearing this type of statement, I struggled a lot and studied day and night as I used to do during the 10th exams. Then the 12th exams had passed.

After some days the results came out, then I got a call from the same physics faculty then he said could you please send me your mark sheet as you topped in the school. This was a very exciting moment and a turning point for me. I found that if I want, I can do anything; I just need to put efforts sincerely.

That's how I had ended my school life..!

After the 12th exam, I joined a crash course for one month for Pre-Engineering Test preparation as I targeted to join the most famous university in the town. After preparation, I had appeared on the PET exam. When the result came I got to know that I was getting marks for getting my targeted college.

[1]

Engineer to be

2011-2015

As I had already decided to take admission in ITM Universe (1997) so worked less for getting it. In August 2011, I started attending classes in CSE-1 Newton block with my cousin.

One day when I was attending computer labs where a task to create a doc file with your information was given to all my classmates. So, I had created and written my phone number along with all my information.

The next day some other branch students came there for the lab. Then one guy took my no. from there. Then he texted me (how silly I was?). So, I met with that guy and that's how I got 1st friend in ITM. He was very good in his English speaking skills. Those days, I was a noob.

Based on his English that guy used to say that you will fail in semester exams because you couldn't write in the exams without a good knowledge of English.

In one of the semesters, we had one subject as basic computer engineering. As this subject was related to computers so it was very new for me. As this guy became my friend so he used to teach me computers. In the first semester, he used to help me a lot. Along with that, he used to come by his dad's car to impress me.

So, we all appeared in first semester exams and that's how I had passed. After some days the results were out and I got to know that I had passed in all the subjects.

As being a student of computer science and engineering, I needed to be proficient in basic programming languages which were not semester subjects but still, we needed knowledge of programming. For programming languages like C, C++ & JAVA I joined classes from outside for learning the codes and becoming the coder.

One day while I was in my C class, I saw my schoolmate Sriya. She also saw me just after seeing me. She called me loudly, everyone else could hear it. So we both met again and discussed all past stories. After meeting again, she had become the answer book of my questionnaire. Whenever I was having doubts, I reached her and collected all the information.

As I was learning codes so for executing and compiling those codes, I needed a laptop. So I asked my dad as I needed a laptop for my further work. Please help me. At that time one thing which my dad could give me, however I expected, was his money.

I made so much research on which laptop I should purchase and in that era which was the best one. So I decided to purchase a laptop with the latest processor in it. So finally I got my laptop with an i7 processor. At that time, It was the first thing in my family which I had best.

After dad's hard work, we came into the upper-middle class from the lower middle class. So things were becoming fine in the family and those days I used to have money in my pocket given by dad. I was chilling in my college life like a rich fellow.

Ram: First Human Being I ever met

Then in the second year, I met one guy and his name was Ram and later I got to know that he was my school senior too. After meeting and talking with him we realized that we both used to stay in the same colony too but we didn't know this before.

After some months, Ram had become my best friend and we had started talking on calls almost once a day. Then one day mom and I were alone at home and my room ceiling fan wasn't working then Ram came to my place and removed the fan from the ceiling and then went to the electrician shop and gave it for fixing.

We had started tagging each other in FACEBOOK posts then the public had started assuming us GF-BF but in reality, we were good friends. So, we used to laugh after reading people's comments on our posts.

I still remember, on my birthday, Ram gifted me one photo collage frame. What he did was he selected some of my pictures which I had uploaded on FACEBOOK, he just collected and made a collage and gifted me that frame. It was the best gift ever as I always wanted to have my pics in one big frame.

During college, we used to talk about our crashes with each other. Like if I saw someone and I liked him by face and Ram saw some girl and he liked her then we used to talk about all that nonsense.

First time in my life after my family I found someone who was this much ancillary and availing man. I really relished him as a person. Every time whenever I needed him he used to avail himself of my help. He never said no to anything.

He had become akin to my family. I must say that he was such a great human being in my life. He had done an abundance of things for me like family, so I used to revere him a lot.

At that time, I was a highly active girl so I used to get proposals from boys. Because of those proposals sometimes I was happy and sometimes I was sad. In the end, I used to tell Ram all the stories and we used to laugh. Every time I used to tell Ram one thing only.

Me: Ram, as you are my best friend like a family. Please never try to propose to me.

Ram: I will never do that because I don't like you at all.

Me: Thanks a lot for not liking me.

But one day something happened with Ram and he got influenced by some of his friends then he crossed his limits which I had set for friendships and he proposed to me. He did the same mistake for which I had already asked him "never to do"

Me: Ram, you shouldn't have done this as I already asked you never to do this.

Ram: Everyone already thinks that we are gf-bf then what's the issue if we are becoming real.

Me: But Ram, we had already set our limits.

Ram: So what, we can break those, because we only made it. It has not been written on stamp paper.

Me: But you have spoiled our friendship.

I tried my best to make Ram understand the things but he was not getting anything. After that, we had a big argument on this. Then we broke our friendship and left each other.

After some months, one notification with my name came on the ITM Confession page. ITM confession page was a page on Facebook at which anyone can say anything without showing their names. In that people used to write something to someone. That notification was written for me with a Hindi song in it.

After seeing this, it clicked into my mind in one second that this was written by Ram. Then we again connected as I got to know that he was very sorry for his deeds. So we restarted our friendship. I would appreciate him as he made things normal between us.

It's 2012 (as we know all leap years are not so good). In ITM, I had a group of 7 years girls, so we all used to chill together inside and outside of the campus. Once one of our friends had a birthday so I ordered a cake and wanted to her to cut the cake but some of the classmates denied for this so we just kept cake and took an auto and we all 7 girls bunked the classes we just kept the cake in the back seat of that auto and asked the auto driver to take to the city mall then we were going on while feeling like a road trip as we girls were singing songs in the auto. After some time we reached the Mall and we all got down from the auto.

After that, we all went into the big bazaar and purchased one T-shirt for each of us then changed because we all were in the ITM uniform. Then we went to the food court.

In the food court while we were talking, suddenly our b'day girl noticed something which none of us didn't.

B'day Girl: Hey girls! Where is my cake?

Me: I kept it in the auto.

Other girl: I think it was at the back of the seat.

Me: Yeah, I also remember this. Then who picked it from there.

cousin: I think no one.

another girl: We left the cake in the auto itself.

B'day Girl: Let's check if the auto is still there so that we can take our cake.

Me: Let me check this from the window itself.

Yeah, the auto left with our cake. Then we all had food in the food court and played some small games. After having food, we all came out then decided to go somewhere.

After all the discussions, we all girls went to the Sindhiya palace. Just in a few minutes, we reached there. Then, we visited it from inside and so many historical things and all the Sindhiyas family pictures and paintings there. Then we saw a dining table in that one train with food trays running so it was really nice to see that. After wandering every corner we all came out of the palace. In front of the palace, we all sang a song and then we recorded the video while singing. We all were dancing together by holding each other's hand and singing one friendship song in a mild voice. It was great fun with the girl gang. We all enjoyed it a lot.

In 3rd year, I went to Indore for my industrial training. There, I joined HCL for my training. They had conducted one interview and I passed that then I joined designing android applications. As for designing android application Java programming language knowledge requires so I had that that's why I joined it. After joining I used to have some 3 hours class only and the rest of the day I had started getting bored. What I did was, I joined for one course that was related to Linux. So I had started working on both projects and also. Life was going on there. After some days, Ram came with another senior to visit Indore. Then we all planned to go to Nakhrali Dhani.

Nakhrali Dhani belongs to Rajasthani and Malawi culture and presents before the visitors a never-ending charm and magnificence to imbibe them into the celebration. Every evening, the resort looks decorated as marvellous as that of a typical village exhibiting Rajasthani traditional elements. Beginning with a warm greeting at the entrance by *aarti* and *kumkum*, the royal treatment further fills the visitor an elated sense of excitement through a funfair like environment. It inculcates traditional dance performances by Rajasthani dancers, entertaining Puppet shows, Bullock Cart Rides, Camel ride, magic show, Horse ride and indeed a sumptuous Rajasthani meal. The village resort also includes- a clean and hygienic swimming pool, a dance zone and a separate dining hall with low rise sittings and affectionately served food. The mouth-watering cuisines served in the large dining hall are a treat of a lifetime. The royal welcome, a humble serving of food in the style of Manuhar and the blend of love and kinship into the served cuisine itself works as the soul-satisfier.

We all went there and booked one package which had included Artist Performances, discotheque, welcome drinks (jaljeera) and one-time meal (lunch/dinner).

So Just after entering we welcomed and got welcome drinks. It was looking like a small village in Rajasthan. So we were watching shows. At one place one magician was showing his magic tricks. From the audience the magician picked me then he kept some coins in my palm and asked me to hold them by closing them. Then he said some mantra for some time then he asked me to open up and then there was no coin. He had started saying you stole my coins that I gave you some time before. I was totally lost like where the coins had gone. I couldn't even think. After all this nonsense, the magician shook my jeans and coins came out. First time I saw magic like this. We all were laughing and the public was clapping.

After this, we saw one woman dancing on the glasses. Then one small girl was walking on the rope which tied at 2-different poles only. It was really horrible but they were looking so professional so we were enjoying it.

After all this, we went for lunch. We all needed to sit on the floor but with that, they were providing one small table for keeping the food on. In lunch, they were providing 56 types of items and then one waiter came to us and he was keeping one laddu directly to our mouths instead of serving it on the plate. Along with food, they were offering pure ghee. It was the most lovely lunch I ever had. I really liked the way they were serving.

After having lunch, we all went outside and there also we were checking a few things and the day was about to be completed. So we all came out and left for our places by taking the city buses of different routes.

After some days my industrial training got completed. As I had completed 45 days there, I collected both training certificates and projects. At the same time, Ram also planned to go home then he only booked train tickets for Gwalior.

Before leaving I just called Ram and said:

Me: Hey Ram, it's been raining since morning and I was fully occupied with my industrial training certificate collection so I couldn't even eat anything. Could you please come with some food which we can eat on the train as train food is not good.

Ram: It's very hard to find food on such a rainy day but don't worry I will try.

Since we had to train in the evening then it was heavily raining that day. After a lot of struggle anyhow we reached out to the railway station.

Ram came with one food package. Then on the train when I opened it, I found aloo paratha as I asked him to buy some food and he bought one of my favourite foods. Then he told the whole story of how he got this food after searching here and there. After eating we finally sat in our seats on the train.

After some months, I had completed my graduation and just after the final semester exam I just left for Delhi to join Made Easy for preparing for GATE. Yeah at that time no one was there to help me so I just did a lot of research to get to know about this coaching centre.

[2]

Love Story

2013-2016

When it comes to love stories, then at teenage everyone has their own story. At a certain age, we all start getting infatuated with the opposite gender. We used to call it love. Love is the best feeling in the world: According to lovers. Every lover thinks that their story is the best love Story ever.

As being an unwanted child of my parents every time I tried to find love in the outside world. I was only looking for love and a person who can adore me. At that time my parents were so busy with their jobs and mom cared about my younger brother so she was busy with him only. I started feeling lonely and Whenever I wanted to share something with someone, I was not even getting anyone to listen to my things. Because in my family no one was interested in my life. Most of the time I felt low confidence as I had developed this feeling because of my circumstances.

In the decade of 2005-2015, everyone wanted to become a doctor or an engineer only. When I was getting anyone from any IIT or NIT which were the top engineering institutes and If someone was doing good in that field then I was getting highly impressed with that person.

The year 2013

One day, I was just using Facebook & I received one friend request but before accepting the request I dropped a message

"Why should I accept your friend request?"

Then after some time, I got a reply from that guy:

"You should accept my friend request because you like me and the same here."

Guy, whom I didn't even know & he replied like this after reading his reply I was shocked & was thinking syncing with him would be quite interesting so just started having conversations with him. Slowly we started talking and came to know about each other. Oh, I forgot to mention his name. His name was Arman. One day what happened I was just listening song:

kitne armaan maan maan maan jaage tere vaaste soniye....

Then suddenly my cousin entered my room and said:

Oh, that's why you used to listen to this song because it's related to your Arman. After hearing this I was laughing with pink cheeks.

After one month of conversations and discussions over the Facebook messages finally Arman asked me for my number. Then we exchanged our numbers. After all, the establishment and conversation love story was going fantastic and we were enjoying our calls.

Love means desiring happiness feeling motivated. If you are in love you are driven to be compassionate, generous & caring to your special someone.

As we were talking and chatting on phone itself but one day Arman expressed something

Arman: Hey, Neel I want to see you.

Me: Yeah, I also want to see you but how?

Arman: Let's set up a video call via Skype.

Me: Ok! Let's do it but for that, I need to do some configuration on my laptop so give me some time.

Arman: Ok, Neel, no problem let's do it on Sunday.

Me: fantastic, I am so excited. I will be ready at that time.

Sunday came and we set up a video call. While he was in a black IIT jacket and I was in my pink winter suit. After seeing me in pink color, he started calling me Pinky. I was very scared before the call but when I talked with him I found him a good enough and cool person.

Initially, I was so depressed as I didn't get any call or message from Arman. So I was fighting with him without saying what I wanted. every time whenever we are fighting or arguing the first thing which I used to was blocking.

Me: Don't message me, else I will block you.

Arman: I will come there and slap you.

Me: How dare you speak to me like that?

Arman: I can speak because I am all yours only.

Me: No, because I hate IITians.

Arman: I hate *Gwar* people from Gwalior.

Me: I am not a heroine so stop being stuck on me.

Arman: Am I looking like fevicol to you?

Me: Stop irritating me, where is your ego now?

Arman: Buried with eggs.

Me: I hate you. Goodbye!

Arman: Listen to me, I am not kidding. I love you.

By this note every time he tried to pacify me. So everything was normal and I didn't expect anything. But later I got to know directly. He came to meet me and surprised me. He came to my place by travelling 777 kms from his place to my place. Yeah, that's because of love. At that time, I was completely blank about how to show my love, how to adore my love. As I never had this feeling of love before as no one ever did anything like this for me. The first time someone was doing something for me and my happiness.

Day:1 (First Date)

According to all plans, as we never met before this, we decided to make our first meet special, so we planned a date. It was my first time going on a date, so I was so excited about it. We decided to meet at Alfanzo restaurant. Well, this is based on the scientific name of mango which is Alphonso. We both used to seek logics everywhere. So, we decided to meet there at 7:30 pm.

Just before leaving for the restaurant, I got a call from Arman and he was asking me

"Tell me Neel after meeting things will be the same among us"

The way he asked & what he asked was the world's best questions with thousands of emotions.

Then in an adoring way I replied:

"Don't worry, Arman, nothing will be changed between us as I love you from my soul to your soul."

I reached the restaurant on time and waited for him although I have already asked him to come on time but he was new to my town so I could accept this. Finally, I saw a man in a black shirt looking like Arman. He entered the restaurant and then we went to the first floor which he booked for us. I was following his steps over the route and then we reached the hall of the first floor where we could feel pin drop silence.

No one except the waiter was in the hall. As a gentleman, Arman just pulled the chair then suddenly I said I would like to sit on the opposite side, not this side (silly me was a big fan of cricket at that time) from that side I was able to watch Television and match on that so chosen that.

We both were so excited and a little scared about the consequences after the date. Lots of happiness could have been seen on our faces. Just as we settled down one waiter came and flamed a candle which was kept at the middle of the table in between rose pellets. Then they started playing slow romantic music. Everything was looking like a dream for me.

Though we both were so scared, we anyhow tried to talk with each other. Then after having a conversation for some time, we started looking into the menu as needed to order something good and tried to feel comfortable with each other. So, after discussing we have decided to order:

- Achari Paneer Tikka

- Chocolate shake

After a few minutes, a waiter came with a tray in which a burning paneer tikka with a lot of smoke was kept on the banana leaf. After seeing their horrible style of serving we laughed a lot as we both were already scared.

I sat at the side from where I was able to watch television in which they were playing cricket. At that time alfanzo staff members were playing a match and those days I was a dying heart fan of cricket. There also I was trying to watch the match.

I couldn't look into Arman's eyes because I was very nervous while talking with him as it was my first time while I was meeting with a boy like this.

After eating, talking and spending some time with him we planned to leave the restaurant. As I went alfanzo by my TVS Streak, I first dropped him at his friend's place that came in between my route. After that, I reached my flat.

After coming back, we both talked on call for a while then we went to sleep by saying good night to each other. When I came to my bed, I wasn't getting sleep. Then I went to my cousin's bed and shared everything with her. I told her I am not feeling sleepy after meeting Arman then she said:

"A *person cannot sleep either that person is so happy or so sad.*"

Yeah, I was so happy everything was looking perfect in my life at that time. So, one day ended like this.

Day:2

On day1, we planned to go for a walk the next morning at 6:30 on a hill near my place. So, I woke up and got ready then went to Arman's place then picked him then reached that hill which was full of greenery from its top. We could see a fantastic view from its top.

We were just walking there and exploring things. Then suddenly I saw a butterfly, so I ran to catch that. By seeing this, Arman just unlocked his phone and started capturing that in a video where I was trying to catch the yellow adorable butterfly.

After this, we saw some stairs going down from the top of the hill, so we came down through those stairs. Just after the end of the stairs, we got one highway road. For some time, we just walked on that highway. Then we needed to come up as we parked streak at the opposite side of that hill from where we came. He just lifted me in his arms and climbed up stepwise. I was feeling so happy and relating that to the movie *Chennai Express* in which Shahrukh Khan lifted Deepika in his arms.

In the evening, we planned to go to a cafe coffee house with all my friends and Arman. At that time CCD was near my flat in the silver state. So I went there with my friends and Arman also reached with his friend. Just after seeing Arman, one of my friends came and whispered in my ear. Just marry him. After hearing this I was smiling with red cheeks. We were all five members and we ordered the same drink. It was quite funny. So we all were laughing.

After the coffee treat, we all planned to go for dinner. Then there was a restaurant in the city centre nearby CCD so we went there. So all my friends were laughing at us as we were the only couple in that group at that time. We enjoyed it.

So, the day came when Arman was about to leave for his place. He had his train in the evening of that day. Just before his train timing, he came to meet me with a bouquet and a beige color teddy in the shape of a rabbit which has a light green ribbon in its neck and a book by Brian Tracy.

I still remember when he was about to give me a bouquet then he said "please take it because I cannot propose to you here."

After some days, Arman asked me to come to visit his IIT campus by joining an industrial visit from the portal. So I also planned the same. Later, he said don't come due to some reasons.

Me: Hey, I am so excited. I really want to come there and visit your campus.

Arman: It's not safe to come here as a landslide happened nearby campus.

Then thoughts came into my mind. Maybe this guy found someone there so he wanted to hide that that's why he was making stories and not allowing me to come there. He was cheating on me. After seeing all the pictures in my mind I replied to him.

Me: Go with your other options, with those stupid girls who give you extra attention. Goodbye!

Arman: I came to meet you by leaving my home food. So you will have to compensate for that.

Me: Please leave me, I am requesting you.

Arman: Hey Neel, I feel so much comfortable with you that's why I do such stupid things and feel so good.

Me: Could you please stop messaging me after this.

Arman: Neel, it hurts when you say like this.

After hearing this, we both sorted things and ended our drama. Then we started planning for further things. I was asking him if he needed something. Then we started discussing some maths problems as Arman was very good in aptitude and reasoning.

2nd Meeting (Valentine's Day)

Love month (Feb) was about to come. This time Arman came on Valentine's day. Let me explain more about this day. Valentine's Day, also called Saint Valentine's Day or the Feast of Saint Valentine, is celebrated annually on February 14. It originated as a Western Christian feast day and is recognized as a significant cultural, religious, and commercial celebration of romance and love in many regions of the world.

Arman came to surprise me on valentine's day but he didn't know that I already left for my hometown as the next day had mom and dad's anniversary (silver jubilee). But after coming he got to know that I am out of town then he only got surprised by this.

Then after mom dad's anniversary celebration I left for town and then after 3 hours travelling, I came back to the town. Then just after coming back, I met with him.

Me: Hey, what do you like most?

Arman: I like rice pudding (kheer) a lot as my mom used to make it when I was in school.

Me: Would you like to eat if I make it for you?

Arman: But you don't even know cooking, how will you make rice pudding.

Me: Let me try it for you.

After knowing that I wanted to try something for him he was so happy and told his friend too. At my flat, at 10:30 pm when all was done with dinner then I went into the kitchen and started the process. I started chopping almonds and boiling milk then I kept rice in that and after sometime kept sugar according to and put chopped almonds in that.

After all this boiled it for 10-15 minutes, I set an alarm for 2:30 am so that it could get cool and when I came back I could keep this in the fridge.

But at 2:30 am when I came then I saw that rice purring had become like a stone then I started crying and went back to sleep. All together those chopped almost were looking so worse in the rice pudding.

The next morning, my family helped in making rice pudding from the rice stone. Then in the afternoon I went and offered rice pudding to Arman and he liked it and appreciated me.

In the evening I had my class maths and reasoning, so he came with me and attended class although he was good at maths & reasoning.

After this, we made a good plan of visiting a few tourist places in the town together. So just made a list & started for it.

1. Gwalior Fort
2. The Jai Vilas Mahal
3. Gwalior Gurdwara
4. Gwalior Zoo

Let me explain about the places which we had visited:

We went to Gwalior Fort, a hill fort near Gwalior, Madhya Pradesh, India. The fort has existed at least since the 10th century, and the inscriptions and monuments found within what is now the fort campus indicate that it may have existed as early as the beginning of the 6th century. We clicked so many pictures in front of the fort and then we waited for the evening sound and light show. It was a 45 minutes show in that through sounds and light the whole story was narrated like now it was constructed and what happened before and after that.

The next morning we went to Gwalior Gurdwara. A gurdwara is the Sikh place of worship and may be referred to as a Sikh temple. So, we went there. Arman was from a different religion and he used to follow his religious activities strictly. Because of this, I was assuming that he won't come inside the gurdwara. But he did not even come inside; he prayed with me. That was really awesome while sharing that moment with him.

After coming out from gurdwara we entered the zoo as it was nearby. At that time Gwalior Zoo was a small zoo in a garden-like complex with a range of animals, from snakes and birds to a white tiger. We both ate ice-cream and Panipuri outside the zoo at chopati.

In the evening, we went to the Jai Vilas Mahal, also known as the Jai Vilas Palace, a nineteenth-century palace in Gwalior, India. It was established in 1874 by Maharajadhiraj Shrimant Jayajirao Scindia Alijah Bahadur, the Maharaja of Gwalior. It was really great while spending time with him like this.

That's how a love story was going on and we both were enjoying precious moments of our life. After spending time together I started falling for him so badly. This was the lovely phase of my life in which I was living. We used to have small fights as we know fights are good for a healthy relationship. One day, one of my cousins tried to manipulate him for seeing his reaction:

Cousin: Hi Bro!

Arman: Neel, what happened to you? Why are you calling me bro?

Cousin: Bro, I am Neelima's cousin. She is sleeping so I want to tell you something.

Arman: Oh! you are in 9th standard na. Ok, tell me, please.

cousin: Yeah, 9th. Actually, Neelima di is very tense that's why she is with me today.

Arman: Why? Has something happened? Can I call now?

cousin: Whom do you want to talk to? With mamma or Neelima di.

Arman: Obviously Neel, do I have to die after talking to your mother.

Cousin: Don't take tension, mamma knows about you.

Arman: OMG! Seriously, she knows me.

Cousin: Yeah! I need to say Neelima di was sharing her dream with his senior.

Arman: What exactly was she saying to her senior?

cousin: Actually one of the seniors of Neelima di, proposed to her today. Then Neelima di told herself single and they both are planning to run away somewhere on mountains in between icebergs.

Arman: Yeah she was single for the last 2 days but not now.

cousin: Please don't tell anything to Neelima di, that I told you about that. Please do something.

Arman: Thanks for letting me know. I will handle situations according to me.

cousin: Neelima di made a good plan with her senior. She is about to cheat you.

Arman: Nothing like that. I know she loves me and that is enough for me. Could you please ask her to talk to me?

When Arman wrote the line, "I know she loves me and that is enough for me" I just took my phone from my cousin and started talking with him. After this incident, my cousin and I came up with zero doubts about Arman's love.

I was in full love mode. So, I used to send him small-small gifts at his college address through Indian posts. Once I sent him the Taj Mahal miniature as a "symbol of love".

After final exams, I did all the research and then left for Delhi as I wanted to join Made Easy Gate coaching because I want to study in IIT for my masters.

After that, we met in Delhi as we joined Made Easy for GATE classes. I joined Ber Sarai centre for CSE and he joined Kalu Sarai centre for ECE.

But when we both came to NCR & stayed in the same town then we used to meet on weekends and used to go for visiting places like lotus temple, Qutub Minar, Jama Masjid, Red Fort in the town.

[3]

You Are Zero

2016

By Fred Rogers "Love isn't a state of perfect caring. It is an active noun, like a struggle. To love someone is to strive to accept that person exactly the way he or she is, right here and now."

In my story along with all the fun, Arman and I had started knowing a lot of things about each other. Then after some days, I found him a totally different person than the person whom I met on FACEBOOK and used to talk over the calls.

After one year of preparation, we both got our GATE results then he got rank in thousands and I just got qualifying marks and couldn't even get IIT with that score. Some days had passed then I found Arman's behavior had been changed for me and one day when we had an argument that he screamed at me and said:

"Who are you in front of me? You are just a zero"

Something that hit me and my self-respect harder.

Every time I assumed myself an extraordinary girl. Since my childhood, I had always given expected results and suddenly someone came and called me zero just because of one exam result. He didn't even look at my caliber, my capability for doing things.

It's like you respected someone most whom you loved most, and you were fully dedicated towards him. One day he came and called me zero. Where all love has gone where all respect. Is this the way of loving someone according to him?

"You are zero" was the statement which I can never forget. A boy from a new IIT who didn't even get placed was talking to me like this. For me, if you can't respect your love then you're not my cup of tea.

After that, I had started feeling broken, sad and depressed. Then my brain wasn't working. Altogether my GATE, As I came to Delhi for GATE preparation and I didn't get good marks. I was not even getting into IIT with that gate score.

On the other end, my love also called me zero. So, I broke up with him also. I remember I just went to his place and threw all his gifts at his face.

This was the worst part of my life; I never expected this guy would talk to me like this. But it happened and due to my bad gate result, no one was talking from the family. So, I got frustrated.

Finally, I came to a critical situation in my life where I was out of mind. As always, my parents stop talking to me whenever I am in the worst situation or come up with bad academic results. All together the boy whom I loved most called me zero.

"You are zero!"

These three words were the worst phrase I ever heard in my life from my loved one. So it hit my self-esteem it hit me deeper than ocean depth.

For me, self-respect is the most important thing so what I did packed all his gifts and went to his place and threw all the gifts on his face. That was the toughest thing for me but I did.

Everywhere I was telling my failed love story and crying in front of everyone then I got one of my made easy classmates who told me about something and that worked for me. So I took a big step.

[4]

One Big Step

2016

One big step I had to take for pieces of my life:

1.   My parents were not even talking.

2.   I failed in my 3 years relationship.

3.   I didn't get a good GATE score.

At this point, I couldn't fix all the broken pieces of my life. I was in the worst situation. Everything was looking zilch. Where to go and what to do was my biggest concern.

I had been crying for the last six months and didn't find any way of escaping from this. Something weird I had started doing was sharing my story with everyone. One day when I met one of my Made Easy classmates, he suggested to me about a meditation centre.

My friend suggested that I should go to the VIPASSANA Meditation center then I did all the necessary research and kept the new DP, packed bag and left for VIPASSANA for healing my pain.

After knowing from him, I googled and found all the necessary information about the **Vipassna** meditation center, which was introduced in India in the 1970's by S.N. Goenka.and after getting all the information I registered myself for one slot of meditation that was a twelve days session.

About the course

The vipassana meditation course is a 10-day silent residential program that focuses on observing the breath and bodily sensations.

So for this 10 days course, I got registration mail and I got a chance to join the course. So after that, I just kept a meditation woman pic in my WhatsApp profile picture. Then I left for the Sohana centre of vipassana before going. I talked to my brother and told him

I am going to the meditation centre so don't tell anyone.

So after this, I left for the meditation centre. It was like running somewhere without telling anyone. So this was the biggest step of my life.

I took a cab from my place to where they asked about the bus so I reached there and I saw some other people also. We all waited for the bus.

After waiting for some time, the bus came and by taking that and travelling for 30-40 minutes, we all reached the centre.

Just after reaching, we received our rooms and they asked us to give them our mobiles. So we all submitted our phones. Yeah, I got room no. 30. We all got plates and food according to our numbers.

I got my plate at stand 30 then I picked my plate, had the evening snacks then we all women left for the meditation hall.

In the meditation hall, with one big projector screen on the left side, I could see all gents and on the right side all ladies. We all sat in a row. There is also the same number of seats as mine was 30.

At the stage, below the projector screen, I could see two dictators sir for all gents and ma'am for all ladies. After this, we all got to know about a schedule that we needed to follow for the next 10 days.

So that's how the schedule had been given and it had started from the first day itself.

4:00 am - wake up

4:30 am - 6:30 am - meditation

6:30-8:00 am - breakfast

8-11am - meditation

11-1pm - Lunch

1-5pm - Meditation

5-6 pm - Tea and snacks

6-7 pm - Meditation

7- 8:30 pm - Lecture

8:30-9 pm- meditation

9:30 pm - sleep

10:00 pm - lights out

The first day itself I got to know that here I would not get dinner. I didn't notice while I was reading details before registering myself. My mistake was not reading the doc file carefully.

So what I had in my bag with clothes and necessary stuff was a Bourbon biscuit and a pen without even a single piece of paper.

So every day I was eating one or two or half of the biscuit because I needed to stay with that single packet for 10 days. So I was eating when I was feeling so hungry because I had a habit of eating dinner before.

I never stayed without books before so after two to three days I had started feeling I should read or write something. So the question was where to write. Then I went out of my room in the garden where I found some big leaves so I picked those leaves and came back to my room and started writing on those leaves by days.

After 4-5 days, I have started feeling that this is a time waste so I wanted to come back and I was still looking fully depressed but ma'am talked with me and convinced me to stay there for some more days. She tried to make me understand the procedure and its advantages.

Ma'am convinced me to stay for two more days but after spending two more days I had started feeling good so I stayed for all the days and completed the course and learned techniques for focusing on breathing. That technique helped me to improve my concentration power.

11th DAY:

On the 11th day, we all went for morning meditation. Then we got to know that the course had been completed. Now we were allowed to talk and finally, silence had been broken. so we all had started talking with each other. Then I met so many women and heard about their motive for coming here. After breakfast, we all got our phones.

So finally I got my phone back. Just after getting mobile I turned it on and called my mom and dad. After hearing their voice after 10 days I literally had started crying even though we all hated each other before coming there. Literally, that was my first day in life when I felt that much attached to my parents.

After that, I just talked with all my neighbors and companions, so I shared my stuff and some other members also shared their stuff. That time one auntie came and said how did you be able to stay here for 10 days because my son left after 2 days. So I laughed loudly and felt satisfied after listening to this.

So that's how my big step became one of the best decisions of my life. I learned a lot of things and applied them in my daily life. That's how I became a "karma believer".

[5]

Karma Believer

2016

Karma is all about what a person has done, is doing, and will do. My dad used to tell us "Do your duty without thinking about results."

Karma is not about punishment or reward. It just makes a person responsible for their own life. The theory of karma believers is the major belief of spiritual people.

In my chapter one big step, I learned about karma and karma beliefs. So after gaining experience I had become a karma believer so I had started following karma rules.

I read so many motivational, spiritual and karma belief books after coming back. Then one day I went to a book fair in Delhi and purchased some of the books based on Japanese author Ryuho Okawa books. The works of author Ryuho Okawa, introducing his philosophies on spiritual wisdom and enlightenment to guide readers to personal growth and happiness.

As I had already become a strong believer of karma where I do things while keeping in my mind how it would affect others as well as how it will affect my own karma. I had started thinking about other people's minds like what they would think and say if I say or do something and discuss my stuff with them.

According to me, karma is what you are serving, you will get back one day.

Another rule which I learned was, "BE HAPPY & MAKE ALL HAPPY"

BE HAPPY & MAKE ALL HAPPY

I worked on that theory and started making everyone happy. Every time I tried to do so many things for others to make them happy.

Since my childhood, I had not been a good child. So after becoming a karma believer first I tried to work on the theory of "BE HAPPY & MAKE ALL HAPPY" So I tried to implement this in my life and I stopped being reckless. For that, I had started behaving well with everyone to make them happy and I tried to give my best. Then, in the end, I saw so many good changes in me. So I had started finding my happiness in others' happy faces.

I had started following another fact that everything is decided by nature whatever is happening or whatever we are planning is a way of flowing according to nature.

In the end, everything happens for a reason. Either it is good or bad. If something bad is happening then stop worrying about that because this is also happening for making you good for the other day. Today is not your day but after some time your day will come for sure.

There are so many karma rules which everyone should follow in their lives. Some rules which I had written here:

1. Creation
2. Growth
3. Cause and effect
4. Humanity
5. Responsibility
6. Connection
7. Focus
8. Giving and hospitality
9. Here and now
10. Change
11. Patience and rewards
12. Significance and inspiration

The ideas of causality and essential elements of the theory of karma were being recited in folk stories. For example:

As a man himself sows, so he himself reaps; no man inherits the good or evil act of another man. The fruit is of the same quality as the action.

— Mahabharata, xii.291.22[53]

In the thirteenth book of the *Mahabharata*, also called the Teaching Book (Anushasana Parva), the sixth chapter opens with Yudhishthira asking Bhishma: "Is the course of a person's life already destined, or can human effort shape one's life?" "The future," replies Bhishma, "is both a function of current human effort derived from free will and past human actions that set circumstances. Over and over again, the chapters of Mahabharata recite the key postulates of karma theory. That is: intent and action (karma) have consequences; karma lingers and doesn't disappear; and, all positive or negative experiences in life require effort and intent. For example:

Happiness comes due to good actions, suffering results from evil actions, by actions, all things are obtained, by inaction, nothing whatsoever is enjoyed. If one's action bore no fruit, then everything would be of no avail, if the world worked from fate alone, it would be neutralized."

So, I don't believe in luck. What I think if you have done the right things in your life then nothing wrong can happen to you. If something wrong is happening with you then also you are only responsible for it. Not luck, not god, not your mom dad.

Another thing which I started to follow for everything a perfect time has been decided. If today you are failing then someday will be your day and you will get success. It totally depends on your karma. How you are doing things from your end how responsible you are for yourself and for your deeds.

[6]

The Struggle

2016-2017

As I was struggling since my childhood, because I never got anything easily in my life. So, this is phase of my life:

- After heartbreak.

- After a lot of failures.

- After taking a big step.

- After becoming a "karma believer".

IIITBH Interview

So now I have determined and set some goals after coming from Vipassana. I just got one interview call from IIIT Bhuvneshwar. As I came back, I was full of confidence, so I cracked that interview even though I went there with one day of preparation only.

ISRO Exam

After 10 days, I just had my ISRO exam, so I prepared hard for it. Recently I came from the meditation center where I used to wake up at 4:30 am so I was still in that mode. So, during exam preparation, I used to wake up early and used to start studying at 5 am. The day when I went for the exam was the 3rd of July. In the exam, I performed well and after getting the answer keys I got to know that I was getting good marks and had a good chance of getting an interview call. So, after discussing with my dad I had started preparing for the ISRO interview and didn't take admission in IIIT-BH.

During the ISRO interview preparation, I used to be awake till 7 am as I struggled a lot. I was very confident as every time every day my dad was supporting, motivating and guiding me for further interview preparations. For the interview, I prepared two-three months like this only then after the 3 months result got out and I got to know that I wouldn't have been selected for the interview.

The interview list had started with 138 marks and I got only 137 marks. So, I lost the game by 1 mark. That day I realized the value of "1".

I had started feeling that day was the worst day of my life. After that I got a call from dad then I told him that I didn't get selected for the interview because of the 1 mark. At that time, I was expecting something positive from my dad. But after listening to this, my dad stated to me:

"What have you been doing in Delhi for the last years?"

After saying this he just disconnected the call and didn't even talk to me. After this big failure and dad's words, I totally got broke. I had given my 100% but still, I didn't even select for an interview. Again, I had started feeling like I am good for nothing.

I had one doubt like I tried my best to get it. Still, I was not getting it then how would it be my fault? Why has no one even tried to understand me? Why every time it happened to me only? So many questions I had in my mind. Like every time mom dad had stopped talking to me. In every worst situation, they used to leave me alone.

Mom and dad had one theory: if something bad was happening to me, then it was because of me and my deeds and if something good was happening then it was because of their support and money. I must say they were awesome with their theories. Although here also I was learning a lot of things like you only need to become your savior. No one else would come and save you.

This had also been passed but still, I didn't get a call from my dad although my sister was in touch. After that, I had a few upcoming exams so I tried to forget the ISRO story and again I started preparing for forthcoming exams. In this, I had the UPPCL & BSPHCL exam mainly. These exams were state-specific exams, so I needed to go to Bihar and UP. After some days I got admit cards for both the exams and what I got these exams are simultaneous days like UPPCL was on the 13th and BSPHCL was on the 14th. Then it wasn't possible to appear in both the exams, so I discussed with my friends then they suggested that I go by flight. But before that, I never travelled by flight.

UPPCL

On the 13th morning, I left for Noida as I had my exam center there. Noida comes in UP and It was near to south Delhi, so it had become easy for me. But going from south Delhi to Noida was 2 hours away then writing the exam and coming back because I needed to go to the airport by taking a flight for Bihar as the next day, I had a BSPHCL exam also.

BSPHCL

I went to Patna through the flight as this was my time when I sat in an airplane. As being alone this was quite a struggle and learning part for me. The help of my sister's guidance over the call helped me a lot so I reached Patna and my sister's friend came so I went to her place. Going to Bihar was one of my bucket list tasks so after landing there

I was quite excited. The next day I had an exam so I went to the center and wrote an exam.

After coming back, I was a little depressed. I didn't get a call from the person who used to call me every day during ISRO interview preparation. Well, that's the truth of life where everyone has their own expectations from you. Sometimes expectations kill.

I just got one new friend named Sanchi in the building where I was staying. She came for UPSC exam preparation. It was a really good time and company with her. We used to discuss general issues. One day Sanchi said I had no life experience so I should go for a world tour. So, I can see different things and people so I can learn from them. I can learn more about life and can gain life experiences.

I liked her advice and kept it on my bucket list because I really wanted to travel at least in India. I discussed this with my mom then she said go with your husband. When I asked my dad about the India tour then he said "you are a girl, you can't go alone "

Well, this is our Indian society here we can't blame a single person. It's the mindset of almost every parent.

Then I asked my elder sister if I wanted to go on a world tour. Then she booked flight tickets from Delhi to Pune. So, for New Year's Eve, I went to Pune. During December it was a very low temperature in Delhi but when I reached Pune it was normal temperature there because it's near beaches that's why this type of climate. Then I reached aka's place.

After that, I stayed there for some days and then me and my sister chilled together. Here, I tried 3 new things:

I went to a pub for the first time although I didn't drink.

I visited the beach for the first time with sis and schoolmates.

I went on a solo trip.

After chilling 4-5 days with my sister and her flatmates, I flew back to Delhi. While I was going to my sis place to the airport to take my flight, there I got stuck in traffic and my flight was about to be missed but due to cab driver support anyhow I got that.

Again, I had started my preparation for further exams.

I had appeared in the JNU exam as it was in front of the colony Ber Sarai where I lived during my GATE preparation.

Call from an IIT

In April 2017, I got an interview call from IITBH. As the interview date was mentioned 11th may so my task was to convince dad.

Me: I got an interview call from an IIT, please take me there for the interview.

After hearing IIT in conversation, dad directly got convinced.

Dad: Yes sure, we will go just book the flight tickets.

Me: Are you serious?

Dad: Yeah I am serious, rest we will see there.

After that, I booked flight tickets from Delhi to Bhubaneswar. Dad came to Delhi then we left for the airport as we reached the airport very early so we both were roaming here and there and dad was asking so many questions as he was curious about his first flight. We both were talking and roaming there.

Dad: See! Here, you will find someone who knows me for sure.

Me: Not possible... But why are you so sure?

Dad: Inner voice. My sixth sense is very strong.

Me: No dad, it's not looking possible. In this crowd finding each other is impossible and you are saying someone known to you will come to you.

Dad: Wait for some time and then talk to me.

Me: Okay!

After sometime when we were roaming here and there then suddenly one person came and handshake with dad.

After seeing this, I was in shock about how it happened.

Dad: I already told you.

Dad and I were laughing at this incident. Then we three went to the airport cafeteria and had some food together.

Then we went for our flight. Dad and I reached there at night time after reaching we tried to find a hotel as we hadn't made any pre-booking. After a lot of struggle, we got one worst hotel like we could smell moisture everywhere in the room. We wanted to leave that but we thought it was about one day so let's manage here only.

Anyhow, we tried to sleep and the next morning we left for the IIT-BH campus. It was a little far from the hotel. While we were going we could see fish and fish smell everywhere.

On the campus, we saw so many people came for the interview. Then I appeared in the written test and after some time the result was announced. I qualified written and secured rank 21. After that we had an interview round for that I prepared it there itself with my dad. Since we reached the IIT campus at 8 am and they called me for the interview at 6:30 pm.

I got so tired so I wasn't able to perform well in the interview along with that I got scared by seeing so many people who were about to ask me so many questions. At last, I hadn't got selected. After knowing this my dad was so furious as he came with a lot of expectations.

Then we came back to the room but it was smelling so bad. When we tried to search other rooms we could get any because due to some college counselling all hotels were occupied. Although we had our train in the early morning.

Me: It's smelling so bad. I can't sleep here.

Dad: Same I am feeling.

Me: Then what we will do, where we will go at this time.

Dad: Let's go to the station. We will sleep there on the platform.

Me: Are you serious?

Dad: Yeah, I think so. Rest you tell.

Me: Instead of sleeping here, the platform is fine. At least we will be able to breathe there.

Dad: Ok pack bags, then I'm paying bills and closing it.

After leaving that hotel first we went to a restaurant for having dinner then left for the station. At the station, we found two benches. At first, the platform was crowded but after some time we got a place to sleep there.

First time In my life I slept on a platform. It was a different level experience which I tried although dad was so supportive even though I couldn't qualify for the interview.

Then early in the morning finally we caught the train and came to our seats. As we faced so many things so we discussed this. Along with that, we talked about so many things. We were continuously eating in the train as dad and I both are kind of foodie. Suddenly something came into my Mind. Then I started:

Me: Dad, sometimes I think your son is a more sensible person than me.

Dad: Yeah because you're out of syllabus. Sometimes I also don't understand what exactly you need.

Me: Oh ok. Sometimes I also feel that I am weird!

Dad: So what are your further plans? Because after this I won't give you money for preparation so decide things and move forward.

Me: Oops! Ok.

That's how we closed the conversation and after travelling one night, the next day we reached Gwalior. My younger brother came with *poha* as I asked them to buy for me. Dad got down there itself and I traveled again for Delhi as I had few exams so went there for further preparation.

As dad had already given deadlines so I thought to search for a job for me. Then I applied for some companies through some online portal and after some days I got a call from one company then I went for an interview. Yeah, I was very naive in that field so I was not looking confident but based on my knowledge and academic they selected me, and then they said for confirming yourself you need to pay 1500 rs to us after that we will process your resume and will call you for joining in a week. Then I thought this should be a process for all companies but as dad already had given last time so I didn't have any extra money with me then I requested one of my friends to give me rupees which I will pay back once after getting my first salary. That's how I arranged and paid that amount to them.

But then I waited for their call for 15 days and when I didn't get any call then I went to the same interview location and tried to check there but there was no company or nothing at that time.

So I got to know that I had been cheated on by them. That was the scam for cheating people by showing them fake job offers. I got trapped in that. Then I noticed that many people would advertise fake jobs.

After one more hit, with no more expectation, I simply thought of joining any college based on my gate marks for getting money. As I was GATE qualified then I could avail to get 400/day and 12400 per month as stipend.

So I applied for counselling and chose some of the national institutes for this. Then in July, the result was announced and I got NIT Hamirpur.

[7]

NITH Journey (Learning Phase)

2017-2019

In July 2017, I joined NIT Hamirpur as I wanted to live on hills, so I had chosen that and that was at 3rd place in my list while filling for colleges.

NIT Hamirpur looks like "heaven on earth". This NIT was established in 1986 is deemed a university and judged the best NIT in terms of infrastructure by the world bank.

The campus is on the foothills of the Himalayan mountains. The characteristics of the landscape are strikingly distinct and offer a pleasant and most memorable visual experience. The weather is cold and pleasant and gives you an out of work experience.

At that time I had a small dream of visiting Shimla and so just after joining NIT I went to Shimla with my Delhi friends and NIT roommate. In Shimla, we all went to an amusement park where we did a lot of activities.

So, I planned to go there with my dad to discuss with dad. I booked the bus tickets. I used to move to new places with my dad. So when I was about to leave Delhi I had 12 bags and 3-4 teddy bears so by seeing those stuff dad got angry and kept scolding me all the way. We booked a room in the hotel so we went there from the bus stand after reaching there.

We had a bus at 8:30 pm which would take 10 hours to reach Hamirpur from Delhi. so we were about to reach the next morning. This was my first time when I was travelling these many hours on a bus. But as people say according to time we need to learn how to learn and move forward.

So finally, dad and I with my 12 bags and 3 teddies reached Hamirpur and from the bus stand, we went to a hotel which was already booked by my elder sister aka. I must say she was big and supportive whenever we needed her.

After reaching the hotel room we freshen up and collected information on how to reach NITH then left for it. After reaching there we submitted all the documents and registered me there in the 2017 batch of mobile computing specialization of computer science and engineering. Mobile computing specialization is related to wireless networks and ad hoc mobile computing.

After completing all the procedures, dad and I went to the food court of college for having breakfast. Then we observed it was continuously raining there due to the hilly area and also nothing flattened like DELHI and Madhya

Pradesh where I had been before. There I met one other classmate and here I applied for a room. So, we got room no. 24 at Aravali hostel on the second floor. Aravali hostel was in front of Satpura guest house plus a 2-floor building including ground floor. As we wanted to get the front side room although we didn't get it then dad said that's ok. This is also not so bad. So, I shared my room with another classmate. As we both settled down in that room then our dad had left for home.

At that time I had a small dream of visiting Shimla as I had already heard a lot of things about it. So, my Delhi friend Sanchi came to campus then we booked bus tickets, and then we all left for Shimla.

So, we reached Shimla at night so we reached the room, then freshen up and came out to visit Mall Road (famous) there where we could see only fog during night time. Then we saw a good restaurant there and we planned to go for dinner. Just before entering, I got a call from my grandpa so I was busy on a call and then I tried to enter the restaurant. Then suddenly I felt I hit something.

Oops, there was a glass wall and I tried to enter from it. All People inside and outside were laughing at me and I was also laughing about what I did. Finally, I entered the restaurant and this time from the main door. Then we had dinner and talked about the next day's plan. Then walked on Mall Road which was full of fog. After wandering there for some time we came back to the hotel and slept.

The next morning we all woke up, had a shower and breakfast, then booked a taxi and went to a HANUMAN Ji temple. Before getting down from the taxi, the taxi driver told me to go without specs else monkeys would snatch my glasses. So I removed my glasses and kept them in the taxi itself.

After coming out of the taxi without specs, I wasn't even able to see anything. Another reason is slow rain and fog made it like this. I was with naked eyes. After that, we all went to an amusement park named HIP-HIP HURRAY. In this park, we participated in different types of activities.

1. Valley crossing

2. Commando net climbing

3. Flying fox

4. Haunted house

5. Bungee jumping

We all had a lot of fun there. While we were crossing the valley another was clicking pics. I still have that hanging pic of mine. The haunted house was such a horrible experience we had.

After that, we planned to climb up to Kufri by riding a horse. The first time, I was riding a horse, so I was so scared that I was even crying and screaming. At that time the owner of the horse was saying ma'am please don't shout else the horse would get scared. I asked what about me, I was also scared. My friends were also laughing at me along with other horse riders.

At that time, I was feeling like that day was the last day of my life because one side of the road was a valley and the road was full of wet soil. Anyhow, we all reached up and saw amazing views and apple trees there. That was wonderful so I forgot all my sorrow how I came up. After having a lot of fun, we all came back to college and Sanchi left for Delhi.

Normal days had started after that. Normal days mean classes and chill with classmates on the campus. There I found a group of 2 girls from the same class, so I joined them with my roommate.

In the first semester, I couldn't perform well as I was still preparing for ISRO so I couldn't put all my efforts into semester examinations. We four girls used to go for small trips and also used to enjoy the campus. So, we all spent the first semester like this. After semester exams we all went to our homes. We used to go to Delhi by Bus. When I was travelling by bus, at that time I got my grandpa call.

Last conversation with grandpa

Grandpa: How are you? Where are you?

Me: I am on the bus, travelling to Delhi. Soon I will come to meet you.

Grandpa: Oh is it! At what time in the morning you will reach Delhi?

Me: Tomorrow morning at 8 am I will reach Delhi. I have something to tell you.

Grandpa: oh tell me what's interesting which you want to tell me?

Me: I purchased something for you that is a gift for you from the money which I got in my stipend.

Grandpa: Oh seriously?

Me: Yeah! It has reached Gwalior. Once I reach there I will take it to you.

Grandpa: How much you have spent on that. Tell me I will give you.

Me: No grandpa, this is a gift for you from my first earnings.

After this, we said bye and disconnected the call. The next morning we all reached Delhi. But the next day I had my ISRO exam, so I stayed in Delhi to appear in that.

In the exam again I couldn't perform well. I tried to go with multiple things together so neither in semester nor in ISRO I performed well then dad asked to work for your masters else in the end you could not get anything.

After my ISRO exam, the next morning I had my train for home (morning at 7 am). But I slept and didn't hear the alarm, so I skipped my train but at 10:30 am I was continuously getting calls from my mom-dad, but I was scared so I didn't pick any call. But then I got a call from my relatives also. I picked that call, he was saying your grandpa had gone then thought in my mind someone in the village. But he kept saying your grandpa, your grandpa... Then I said no it's not possible. The day before yesterday I talked with him and told him about the gift (yeah, I purchased a radio for him as he used to listen to commentary and news on the radio).

At last, I got my grandpa, my favorite person for whom I purchased a gift from my first stipend, was no more. Now I couldn't serve him anything anymore.

I ran and caught the train, but it was wintertime all trains were stuck because of the fog. So I reached late, and I couldn't even see him last time. That was a great regret for my whole life.

First time in my life, I lost someone whom I liked most and respected and shared all my NITH Stuffs with him. He used to say, "I am staying in India's coolest place". So, I spent a month at my grandpa's place by missing him each day.

After coming back, I needed to register myself for the second semester like all other classmates. In this semester we needed to take one elective subject from another branch.

I have taken climate change and water from the civil branch. Later, I met another friend while attending class in the civil department of that elective subject. This guy was a 10-pointer guy plus a writer who writes poems. I used to call him Shukle

I had attended some of his stands up although these were so boring for me but anything for friends. And, I found Shukle a good human being. I always respected intelligent minds. Because of this 10-pointer guy we all girls had started going to the library with him and had started studying there.

I always had a good habit of adapting good points from someone's life when I am closer to them and they are good enough.

I was a very straightforward person so I used to say everything in front of everyone as if I am right then I think we shouldn't be scared of anyone until we are not doing anything wrong with anyone.

Shukla used to suggest to me that even if you are still you shouldn't say things directly to anyone as it can make others sad. I try to follow shukle's words.

In NITH, I had three different phases of my life based on different days:

1.   Happening time

2.   Hard time

3.   Horrible time

Happening time

Normal days means following routines and passing days. Every day we used to go for biometric 9:30-10:30 in the morning and 4-5 in the evening. This semester also we had five subjects, so we were attending classes.

Hard time

At the end of this semester, we all classmates were planning to throw a farewell party for seniors. every time everyone was making different decisions regarding parties. After a lot of discussions between all my classmates at one time, I found all the girls are from my side and will support me for all further decisions. But at the other time, I got to know that every other girl in my class was following the boys of the class.

Every time girls try to follow boys instead of taking their own decisions. I really hate this but sometimes we can not make everyone understand everything.

So, finally, I created one WhatsApp group and added all the girls there and then added all the seniors. After that, I discussed them regarding farewell dates. In the starting, they said to tell in some time but then all the boys of classmates tried to brainwash seniors and wanted to convince them for the farewell dates according to themselves. Later, one guy from my class came and started arguing with me and no other girl in the class supported me. even no one stopped those foolish boys. But as being independent and single-handed since my childhood I was able to manage that situation softly although those fools screamed a lot at me.

Because in India everything is male-dominated. when a male sees a woman is trying to make decisions based on her capabilities then they can not digest this. This is because of Indian culture or we can say this is because of their upbringings. They haven't been raised where they were taught to respect humans decisions either it is he or she. We can not blame a single person.

So seniors behaved the same as per expectation. But I wanted the farewell party as soon as we could throw it. Because at that time I had purchased a golden dress for 10.5 bucks. So this dress price had been spread among all the classmates and seniors. Then I talked to so many people about how to convince seniors for some early date. Once a senior suggested asking Sardar ji sir to convince every other senior because everyone listens to him. So I did the same.

I said Sardarji sir, "Could please decide on one early date as we were planning for so many days if possible."

Also, I had added that line "everyone in your class listens to you" so please help me and make them convinced for partying on the earliest date.

So Sardar ji sir said, "Ok, the party would be planned on the earliest date only"

So finally after a lot of struggle I made things possible according to me. Yeah, we had given one name for the party and that was ALOHA. We dedicated ALOHA to saying goodbye to our seniors. But yeah also got to know that no one supports you when you are standing for something. So finally seniors' farewell day came and we all went in our dresses. Finally, I carried my 10.5K dress. It was my first time when I purchased something by paying this much money so I was excited about carrying it. Being from a middle-class family, it was so much. We all enjoyed ourselves a lot at the party as we all danced, arranges so many games for the seniors.

After all this, one day I received one message from one of the seniors as he wanted to discuss something regarding meditation and spiritual flow. As being a dedicated person towards meditation and supernatural things I talked with him then we had started discussing how people think and how to make decisions and all the life-based thoughts and decisions. This senior had become my personal computer. I used to put all my personal thoughts regarding spiritual and human minds. So I gave him a name that's PC which is a full form of the personal computer. Because every time I was treating him like my personal computer.

Horrible Time

After one year, the hostel room and student reshuffling had started. Again, and again hostel admins were calling all students and starting processes and on the other day reverting with everything. I got frustrated with their processes, so I had written one complaint in the complaint register in which I have written as

"Stop doing mental harassment else I will go to the director or MHRD if it's required."

After reading that complaint warden imposed a fine of 5000 bucks for threatening administration. Then again for saving me I have replied with another letter and in that letter, I have written

"As a student, how could I threaten administration!" With this letter, I went to the warden. The warden asked me to go to the chief warden.

I already heard some rumors about the chief warden that he was a womanizer. So, he already had a bad impression. When I was about to enter his cabin, just after opening the door, he looked at me aggressively for a while(like I stole something). So I had started myself:

"I am Neelima and because of one complaint which I had written in the complaint register, I got imposed by the fine of 5000 bucks. What was my fault?"

The chief warden replied as "you tried to threaten administration that's why we imposed a fine on you. Now no one can save you. Even if you go to the PM or CM then also no one will be able to save you. Now you are gone."

Then I came to the hostel and discussed the whole situation with my dad. At that time the only person who supported me was my dad. After listening to the whole stuff, in the end, dad supported me to write to the director. So I had written to the director by pasting everything that happened.

Then I got a quick response from the director and the case was handled by some senior faculties for further investigation. In an internal investigation, all senior faculties were supporting their 10-20 years employees, not me. I could see a conspiracy toward me. So I was afraid and worried if they would rusticate me and my one year would be wasted because of my small complaint.

This time I had written to the PM and CM also. After some days while I was tracking the PM letter, it got stuck at Shimla office due to less connectivity it couldn't come to NITH. Then I didn't get any support.

My BIRTHDAY

But my birthday was about to come and because of all this complaint and case I was so exhausted so for healing myself, I had decided to celebrate my birthday with maximum NITians.

I already received one cake from one of my old friends so before midnight I cut that cake with my trio group in their room. At midnight all the girls decorated my room while I was in some other friend's room so this was a little surprise for me. Then all the hostel girls of my batch came with cake and celebration stuff. so I cut the second cake and then we all danced and chilled for 1-2 hours. After that, we all slept in our rooms.

The next day I picked a packet of chocolate that I already bought to distribute to everyone. Then I left for the department for biometric. In the department, I gave chocolates to whoever I knew like faculties, seniors, batchmates and juniors.

After biometric, I came back to the hostel, then me with my trio friend went to each friend's room, distributed chocolates, and invited them for gathering during the cake cutting in the evening.

In the evening I asked Shukle and all my hostel batchmates to come for a party at the Suraj restaurant so we booked one and reached Suraj restaurant. So we all girls with Shukle celebrated there.

When we all were done with dinner then I went for billing at reception then they gifted me something. Later when we reached the hostel I got to know that it was a coffee mug. I was very thankful for this humble treatment.

After coming back we all gathered in the mess and I received 2 cakes, one from my best friend Ram and another from my sister who pretended to be angry with me. So we kept both the cakes on the table and all the hostel mates gathered then I cut the cake and all were singing happy birthday songs for me. Due to this sound, other nearby hostel people were also started. So the warden came and stopped us. Then silently all girls were putting cake pieces on my face and hairs.

That's how I celebrated my birthday as I always wanted to celebrate my birthday like this and I did that. So we can say all your wishes you're only there to fulfill.

In the end, I got a warning to leave the hostel so I got scared then again I had written to the director as per PC's suggestion. PC was a great supporter and spiritual person in all my worst days in NITH. He was known to everyone as he did his B.TECH and M.TECH. from NITH all together he was my senior as well Himachali.

All the things like investigation and back to back fine letters were looking like real CID episodes of my life. Here I saw many things and learned about a lot of truths of life. When friends turned into enemies and played against me by making a team with attenders.

I realised one thing in the end, only your parents and true human beings can be on your side when you're in trouble. Everything and everyone is fake with a smiling face.

CM LETTER CAME TO NITH

This case was going on. Continuously I was getting letters, calls and inquiries to me. CM letter received by the administration so after some days I got a call from Sinha sir, who was the right hand of the director. That's what the PC told me. Sinha sir asked me to come to his office.

When I went to his place he asked me to settle up the case by paying some small amount so that we could get some respect for our old employees. He almost convinced me of this. As he was very polite to me so I agreed with him. So he asked me what amount you would like to pay then I said only 1000 then he said ok let's make it 1500 and let's close it. Then I also agreed to this. After all this, the administration was furious and was looking only for a single chance of taking revenge.

Placement time

It's July 2018 and placements had been started as I prepared hard for written tests and coding rounds so I had good expectations of getting a place in the first attempt itself. As I was the first candidate from my class who was clearing written with one another classmate and every time I was getting rejected in an interview and another of my classmates was getting hired.

First time I got rejected and the second time Allen coaching institute of Kota came for placement. But this time also the same happened. As I cleared written with another classmate and again I got rejected in the interview and my classmate got hired.

The same thing was happening with me and every time I was getting rejected and one of my classmates who was qualifying wrote with me getting selected. The same thing happened to me till last.

One of my classmates who wasn't even getting a qualifying written test got diverted from the goal and she stopped focusing on placement. But I was still on the same page and along with placements, I had started preparing for GATE 2019. This time also I qualified GATE.

Then one startup company came. we heard a lot about this company as this was related to AI and MACHINE LEARNING so after appearing in 6-7 rounds I got selected for a writing assignment of 30 days of this company. So, I started working on it with one of my Junior. So, after all this company people came to campus for an interview. That day was Sunday so I couldn't write out of the hostel letter although I asked the attendant that I had an interview on the campus itself. The interviewer came at 6 PM so the interview had started at 6:30 pm and it had ended at 10:30 PM. After that, with one security guard, I came to the hostel which took 10 minutes to get back from the training and placement block to Aravali hostel.

So, again the administration played with me and sent one fine letter with a fine of 5000 bucks for me. Although I went for an interview on the campus only and also, I told this to the attendant still they had imposed a fine on me.

I had been hired for this job with a good package. This company was at a Hyderabad location, so I needed to go there for a job.

As getting rejected in 9 interviews, although I had been focused on my goal till last so, in the end, I got a job. In life we shouldn't give up early, that's what I learned from this.

During interviews, I went through a lot of struggles so after getting a job I went to a party at Chopra restaurant with my junior who was working with me on my 30 days assignment. I wanted to pay off him as he helped me a lot during assignment completion. At Chopra restaurant, we had some drinks and because I was so happy, so I had some more pegs by forgetting everything. After that I was continuously vomiting everywhere in the restaurant then they charged for it also.

After all this nonsense we came to campus and still I was looking a little drunk. While I entered the hostel and called myself for attendance in front of the attendant, they got to know that I was drunk. Although after this I came to my room.

But some girls themselves stood against me as we know one girl can never be supportive to another girl so that's what happened with me. When I was in the room and I didn't open it then the warden came, and girls became witnesses for seeing me drunk. Then again, I was imposed with a fine of 5000 bucks.

After some days, I heard one rumor regarding my placement that the junior who helped me during my placement time, because of him only I got this job else I couldn't even get this job. People who couldn't even be able to do anything in their lives were commenting on me like this. At that time I had decided not to say anything because I am a karma believer so believed one day my karma would let them know the truth. So I left that there itself.

At the same time, I heard another thing about me from another junior:

Junior: Ma'am, I want to tell you something about what is your image in juniors.

Me: Ok, Tell me what you juniors think about me?

Junior: We heard one statement from your adjacent junior.

Neelima ma'am is a very rude person who doesn't even talk respectively with anyone.

Me: Oh! what else?

Junior: Neelima ma'am is very rich so she is full of attitude and she is always drunk inside and outside of the campus.

Me: Ok! No problem.

At that time people had this type of perception for me. Well, I couldn't help anyone to let me know. It's their choice how they want to think and how they want to judge me. Although whatever was stated for me, in that nothing was correct.

In the last few days, we had hostel farewells by hostel juniors. In that junior girls honoured me with the batch of MISS MOODY. I was thinking are they honouring or insulting. Well, I was fully drunk so I didn't even care about that. But yeah some speech was also delivered for this as

In the mess, Neelima ma'am used to look in different moods. Sometimes she laughs loudly and sometimes she doesn't even talk to anyone and looks angry. Based on that we chose this tag for ma'am.

Well, I am human so I can not stay with the same things everyday everywhere. Everyday things change according to that mood and human behaviour. The same I was doing.

After the final thesis presentation, faculties were not submitting my thesis. As they were asking me to call your parents and pay the fine then only, they would submit my thesis. So, my sister came to NITH and signed on the fine letters.

After some days when I was waiting for my master's degree but then I got to know that they had denied sending it to me. After knowing that again I had written a letter to the director so that I could get my degree at my job place as I needed to submit there. I got my master's degree and that's how my NITH journey ended where I saw the ups and downs of life and I learned a lot of things.

[8]

Accomplishment

(2019)

Everyone appreciates being recognized for their accomplishments. When someone you know reaches a goal, sending an achievement congratulations shows that you recognize the person's hard work. It is also a good way to stay connected and build a relationship.

People who used to call me insane had started saying:

Yeah, we already knew you would do something like this.

Suddenly, I saw different people with changed opinions for me. There had been many people in my life who had helped me get where I am today. My teachers always supported me in school so I could learn things easily. My parents by being strict and not letting me get into any trouble. In all of my problems, I used to find ways for sorting them out.

My parents are a big reason why I am where I am today. By my parents being strict and tough on me, it helped me a lot. It kept me away from hanging with the wrong crowd.

Because I didn't live in the safest neighborhood in the town. But my parents did it for a reason for my own good. They always kept me busy putting me with books.

"To be yourself in a world that is constantly trying to make you something else is the greatest accomplishment." – Ralph Waldo Emerson

Many of you, like me, have been sitting in a job interview going through the ringer of questions, when you're asked, "What is your greatest accomplishment?"

"What is your greatest accomplishment?" can feel pretty loaded. Do you talk about something personal or professional? What comes to mind? A few years ago I was asked this question and I was totally stumped. I sat there, looking down at a copy of my resume, hoping the answer would jump up at me.

Nothing. Nothing was coming to my mind. Then everything was coming to mind – growing up, moving around, school, graduation, work, I couldn't shut out the overwhelming number of things spinning through my head.

There's just as much there for you. What I ultimately landed on was an answer similar to this:

"My greatest accomplishment is sitting where I am right now. I believe that life is a constant work-in-progress and that all moments, the monumental huge ones and the small quiet ones, all makeup who I am. Being offered something would be another important, meaningful moment that would represent another proud accomplishment in my life that I had been fortunate to experience so many wonderful things.

Our lives are not marked by one significant moment that changed it all. And if you're anything like me, pinpointing the "all-time greatest" moment feels damn near impossible. I asked several of my friends what their response would be and I got answers that included:

- Becoming independent.
- Living my life on my terms.
- Repairing relationships with everyone.
- Finding the way of peace in my life.
- Realizing I have more potential than I thought.
- Rebuilding from a mental breakdown.
- Being able to find ways to learn & grow every day.
- Molding things negative to positive.

That moment – your "greatest accomplishment" will likely change. It isn't set in stone and just as your past doesn't define your future. Be proud of whatever accomplishments you have.

I stayed with my family and we had a lot of fun. As I could feel my mom dad had started valuing me. They used to praise me. I always expected this from my parents, so I had the best part of my life and this was my accomplishment.

So, I went to Delhi, and then from Delhi, we had a flight for Hyderabad. I was going with my dad. We reached Hyderabad then the next day I had an office. The next day on 10th of July at 10 am I reached the office location. Then I saw there's one building of 3 floors and at first the GATE team works. In GATE CSE we used to have 12 subjects, so these subjects were distributed to all mentors including me based on their interests.

I got C, DS and algorithms and I became a mentor of subjects. There we had tasks as follows:

- Talking to students
- Solving their doubts
- Creating questions, which cannot be found anywhere.
- Resolving daily comments
- Writing notes.

In this startup, I used to work 10-12 hours without any break all together. Also, I was not getting the weekend off. So, after some days I was with loads of work and not even getting a proper day off. Meanwhile I met my south-Indian friend, who was one of my old friends as we met on a campus visit.

After seeing me struggling like this, my old friend said,

Old friend: startups just look good in the beginning but, we need to work hard by leaving our life aside.

Me: oh is it? Then let me do some research.

Sometimes accomplishment also looks incomplete so after a few days and having conversations with few of my friends I also started feeling like this.So I concluded this is not the end point, still I need to work for my dream. With the same motivation I started my new journey for a new achievement.

[9]

Dream Comes True

[2020]

As my friend tried to suggest something which I didn't know before, I took his suggestion and downloaded naukari.com and started applying to top MNCs like google, amazon, Microsoft, Facebook.

First, I got a call from Google, so I started preparation for it. But during the interview, when in the 1st round they got to know that I was not doing coding then they stopped my interview and asked me to connect after discussing the team.

Then the second call I got from AMAZON. I went for an interview. In that interview, I appeared in

1st round: DS, C, Algorithm

2nd round: Algorithm question

3rd round: practical algorithm merging

After that, I got disqualified as I didn't answer properly in that round. Yeah then had lunch there then attended the orientation session. In the end, they gave me chocolates then came back home.

Then I left home for the Diwali celebration and it had become very tough to survive in this startup. So still I was applying for other jobs. After coming back home, I just got another interview call that was from Qualcomm, so I went for an interview. Here, they had conducted like:

1st round: Written-test

2nd round: logical reasoning round

3rd round: C, DS & coding question

4th round: Coding

5th round: HR round

After that, I didn't get any calls for some days. So again, I applied for ISRO as the exam was in JAN 2020. Then I left that startup job due to heavy work and unusual manager calls. I got the Qualcomm HR call and he told me,

HR: Hey Neelima, as we all discussed you're selected for this job.

Me: Ok, thanks for informing me.

After ending this HR call, I called my sister and told her

Me: Sis, I got a call from HR and he was saying something like I had been selected etc. I didn't get anything.

Sis: Stupid girl, you are selected for this job role in this company. Just be happy and celebrate it.

At that time, I didn't even know that Qualcomm is this big and top MNC. One day I was on a call with a PC. At that time, I was telling him:

Me: PC, I had a dream of getting placed in the top 4 MNCs Google, Amazon, Apple and Facebook. But recently I gave Qualcomm interviews and got placed in that.

PC said: "Your dream has been completed."

Then I asked: How? Why are you saying this?

Then PC only told me a shocking truth.

PC: Because Qualcomm is also one of the best MNC.

After that he shared some links regarding this then I got to know that Qualcomm mostly hires IIT, NIT students.

Last week of the last month of 2019, I joined Qualcomm so after joining my second life with new things had been started. In Qualcomm, I had started working as an engineer. It had been just a new journey in my life. Here I got a good package too.

So, after knowing the package and about the company my family was so happy, and they were proud of me. This was my biggest achievement like

"DREAM COMES TRUE"

Because I always wanted to be the reason for their pride so that my parents can say in front of society

"Yes, we have 2 daughters and a second daughter is not our unwanted child, with her hard work and patience she has become most wanted."

That day after waiting 17 days finally I received my offer letter, at 1 am after receiving that and seeing the package and all the details I called my sister.

Me: Hey Sis, I finally got an offer letter.

Sis: What they have given you?

Me: I am getting a joining bonus plus a fantastic salary package.

Sis: Oh great! Finally, you got what you deserve. Just call dad he would also be so happy.

It was 12:30 am. When she asked me to call dad. Then my sister and I were so happy and excited to be called dad also without even worrying about time.

So the next morning I called my dad and told him about it. When I was in school at that time getting placed in such a big company like QUALCOMM was only a dream for me even for my family. But today when I got placed in that company then seriously, I felt like my dream had come true.

Before living my dream I just called my NITH junior who taught me some subjects during my placement time and later stated that I got campus placement because of him!

Me: Hey junior as you said in NITH that my job was because of you and you think I couldn't do anything.

Junior: Yes ma'am, that's true and it was me only.

Me: Then keep this startup job in your pocket and I had been hired in the QUALCOMM with my caliber and knowledge and without any favours.

Junior: Ma'am, you can't do. You're lying.

Me: That's real ME! I have more potential and caliber than your fake statements.

That's how I ended things and showed people my karma instead of screaming at them at that time. I got so many calls from my previous classmates too who didn't even like me. But yeah I was doing good so people were coming to me. That's how we humans behave.

I along with my family was so happy as we all never expected that I would have had this success in less time. So now I have started living my dream. My office is near my place, so I used to go by walk as walking is good for your health. As I used to get breakfast in the office, so I used to go to the office to grab it.

After discussing all the sweet and sour memories of my life, Let's come to the present. Today, I am 27 years old. After being one year into the job, it's the year 2020. I have started living my dream, which included a few things:

- I recently rented a flat for myself for staying alone as I have started loving myself and I wanted to stay like this. I have become like a saint.

- I purchased all the household items with my own money. Recently I bought a blue car for myself, without being dependent on others. Along with that, I have become the first girl in my family who has her car.

- Today, I am working for myself, able to make my own decisions independently. All together my family is also happy and finally, *I am my dad's favorite person.*

I never expected in my previous life that I would ever live life like this. It was only my dream of living life like this. But we can say that if you are working hard with determination & consistently then you can get anything in your life.

So I can say that I am living my dream. Yes, today I am a happy, independent and strong woman. Also, I am a strong believer of karma. According to me, if today I am doing something right or wrong tomorrow for sure it will come to me only. So I am only responsible for my today and tomorrow whether it is good or bad.

I don't say anyone has done something wrong with me or anyone is the culprit for anything. It is just Indian society and how people behave and react to things. I don't say my parents have done anything wrong with me, it's just they also went through a lot which I didn't know and because of that they became that type of person. I don't say my parents are wrong, it's just that society made them behave like that. They loved me, and because of their efforts today I am here and able to fulfill all my dreams.

It's not about individuals. If we want to change in our society then we all need to come together. If one is accepting and another is rejecting, the situation can never be resolved.

In the end, I want to summarize this: whatever happens in our lives it happens for a reason and most of the time this reason is supposed to be good. Just work consistently wherever you are and whatever you are doing. No matter what others think, no matter if you're failing, no matter if no one is supporting you, no matter if everyone is laughing at you.

Just give your 100%. Work for you, live for you, do things for you. But yeah never harm anyone and anything. You should do things for yourself without harming others.

Altogether what I have concluded we should not stop anywhere in our life. Like we set a goal and work hard for achieving it and after some time, we are achieving it. Then instead of stopping, we need to set another goal and we should start working for it. We all should work continuously.

According to me a perfect human being is a person who is balancing things in all aspects of her life. We should never stop anywhere and anytime. So after dreaming and making it real I have started my search for my Mr. Perfect. Today, I am not sure whether I will find my Mr. Perfect or not. Although I am working for it. So I have faith in myself. Let's see how my search will go for my Mr. Perfect in the next phase of my life!

In the end, I want to thanks some people:

- Thanks to those who hurt me, you made me a stronger person.

- Thanks to those who loved me, you made my heart bigger.

- Thanks to those who cared, you made me feel important.

- Thanks to those who worried, you let me know that you care.

- Thanks to those who left me, you showed me the meaning of true friends.

- Thanks to those who entered my life, you helped me to become the person I AM TODAY.

Let me know some answers:

- Who am I?

- Will my search for true love end?

- According to you, Am I right or wrong?